Poppy

SARAH LAMB

A thank you to my proofreader, Brooke, and all of the lovely women who help ARC read to catch those typos I miss!

This book was not written by AI. Any typos are proudly (and embarrassingly!) my own human created ones!

ISBN: 978-1-960418-44-9

Contents

To all those who find life has turned out differently than hoped, but still manage to find the beauty it holds.

WELCOME TO GARDEN BELLES
MAIL-ORDER BRIDES

Established in 1850, during the height
of the westward wagon train exodus,
and the various land runs. Men,
desperate for a partner, a wife,
turned to Saint Louis sisters Dahlia
and Zinnia Williams (aka the Garden
Belles) for assistance.

**The sisters, both spinsters, are
especially proud of three things in the
lives: their garden, filled with every type
of imaginable flower; their penchant
for finding perfect wives for most
suitable husbands; and more
importantly, the orphaned niece they
raised from a baby.**

Join us as more would-
be brides are matched
with eager husbands
for their own happily-
ever-afters.

Chapter 1

"Let's see who is looking for love today," Dahlia Williams said, then jumped up as her elbow struck the teapot next to her. Warm amber liquid spilled on the stack of mail and pooled on the small table.

"Oh dear," she moaned. "Look what I've done." She mopped at the spill with a linen napkin. "I've ruined the letters that arrived today! All of these lonely hearts waiting for us to match them with the right person. And I've damaged the ink! Look at it run!"

"No matter," her sister Zinnia answered, coming over with freshly cut flowers in her hands. She set the peonies and snapdragons down into the vase of water she'd already filled and eyed the mail critically. "Accidents happen. I'm sure we can still make out the letters inside. You dabbed it up quickly enough."

"I'm sure you are right," Dahlia said, squinting at a soggy envelope in her hands. "How clumsy I am today!" She laughed then, "I remind myself of Iris! Remember the letter her mother sent us so long ago?"

"There was a dear girl," Zinnia said. "I'm glad that she had a happy ending with our match."

"I am as well," Dahlia said. "We are good at what we do." She shook the letter, and a few drops of tea flew through the air, landing on the grass beneath her feet. "Thankfully, it appears just to be these three pieces of mail that got wet. And it's not likely the insides are unreadable," she added in a brighter tone.

Zinnia sat across from her sister and reached for one of the damp letters. "I'll start with this one," she said, opening the damp envelope carefully.

"My fingers are tingling. This one must be good," Dahlia said happily as she peeled the envelope open. "Let's see what it is."

"Are you sure that tingling isn't a slight burn from the hot water you spilled?" her sister asked. "Do you want some ointment?"

"It's not." Dahlia quickly checked her hands to be sure. "I'm fine. Hmm. Though, this might be a difficult placement, and one for another day. This man wants a wife who can help care for his aging mother and father," Dahlia said with a frown, setting the letter in a pile before taking up the last one. "He also has quite a list of requirements for her."

"That might indeed be difficult," Zinnia agreed. "Perhaps your fingers were tingling as a warning sign. We are matchmakers, not miracle workers." She held up her letter. "Now, this is possible. Mine is a young woman who wishes to marry someone who travels. Oh dear. She sounds so cheerful on the paper, but I can feel her sadness beneath her words. Listen to this. She's an orphan. Skilled with taking care of children, and is open to someone to have a family with, including if they already have children."

"Is that so? This letter here, though part of it got damp and I can't make out all of it, belongs to a businessman who travels a good deal. He has two children and wants someone to help care for them. Why, that checks off everything she's looking for, and him!" Dahlia waved the letter, looking pleased. "Travel, children, ready-made family."

Zinnia smiled. "That's perfect, then. I think we've made a match. And before we're even on our second cup of tea!"

"We are talented like that," Dahlia said. "Shall I write them?"

"Yes, indeed," Zinnia said, handing her sister the pencil that had started to roll away. "It makes me happy that we are able to help love grow in the most unexpected places and between two people who have never met."

Dahlia nodded. "Yes. Only..." she frowned.

"What is it, dear?" her sister asked.

"It's just his letter..." Dahlia bit her lip, then shook her head. "Well, something about it bothers me slightly. He didn't call us the Garden Belles Agency. He called us something else, and I can't quite make out what because the ink ran. Only 'Garden' is legible. He also spends a good deal of time talking about the children, instead of himself."

"I don't see where that matters," Zinnia answered with a shrug. "Perhaps he just wants to make sure he gets a wife who is suitable, and who knows what to expect with the children. Not all are well behaved, you know. We're sending him the woman he needs, we're sending the woman to the man she needs, and that's all that matters in the end."

"You are right," Dahlia answered, and promptly began to pen letters to Miss Poppy Wilson and Mr. Preston Parker, letting them know the future each desired was only days away.

A little thing like a smudged letter surely wouldn't be enough to stop the romance that was destined to happen. After all, since when had either of the sisters ever been wrong in their matchmaking? There was no reason at all to think that this time would be any different.

Chapter 2

Poppy Wilson pushed open the boarding house door and paused at the small entryway table. A collection of envelopes rested on it in a neat stack. The mail was here! She quickly pounced, swooping it up and flipping through the envelopes one by one.

While she wasn't really expecting anything, she sure was hoping for something. After all, it had been almost two weeks since she'd sent off her letter to the Garden Belles Mail-Order Brides. She was most eager to see if she'd get a reply from them.

Poppy had felt a little silly writing to the mail-order bride agency, she had. There was a certain stigma attached to being the kind of woman who couldn't find a husband. But an acquaintance, a whole year younger than her twenty-two, had come into the bookshop where Poppy had been putting out a new display of journals, and excitedly bought one, telling her all about the man she was about to marry and how she wanted to record every moment of her journey to him.

After congratulating her, Poppy had asked who the lucky man was. It turned out to be a wealthy cattle baron out west. And all she'd done was send a letter to a matchmaking agency, asking for the perfect husband!

After the shock had worn off, an idea had filled her mind. Why couldn't she try for the same? She didn't need a wealthy cattle baron, but one never knew! After all, there were many men out there. Who was to say she couldn't also get one who was well off?

Poppy had peppered her friend with almost endless questions then, quite unashamed to be doing so. How had she found the agency? Were her expenses really paid to go West? Would it be possible for her to have the name of the agency that made the match?

That evening after work, Poppy carefully composed her own letter to the sisters who supposedly made the most perfect of matches, according to her friend. In it, she told them about herself, what she longed for, and how she was as untethered as a tumbleweed and quite excited to travel, but she did want someone who would love her, and who she could love.

Then she addressed it, checking multiple times that the address on the scrap of paper matched what she'd written down. It wouldn't do to have it go to the wrong place.

As she'd walked to deliver the letter the next morning, Poppy couldn't help but wonder what kind of man the Garden Belles would find her. If they did. There was the small possibility they wouldn't be able to match her. At least, not right away. But there was no reason that she couldn't have a husband for herself. And soon! After all, the world was vast, and not everyone was already married.

Poppy had always been of an optimistic personality. Which, she had been told, was extraordinarily unwarranted, seeing as life wasn't kind to her. But, it was precisely that fact—that life had been full of challenges—that Poppy was so cheerful, and always seeking the bright side. At least, she tried to.

It was far better than the alternative. Which would be to allow herself to slip into great despair. If she thought too hard or too long about all that had happened, there was the risk of sorrow overtaking her sunshine, and she didn't want that. Couldn't let it happen.

Dreams didn't come true if one didn't have hope in them.

And when it came to her dreams, Poppy had two. The first was to travel. To see the world and all of its wonder and beauty. She'd seen illustrations of mountains and bodies of water so vast one couldn't see where they ended. There were flowers and trees of types she'd never heard of, and animals she'd never seen beyond the pages of a book. There was art and music, architecture and ancient history.

The world was so full of many wonderful things, and she wanted to see and experience as much of it as she could. There was nothing and no one to keep her from doing it, either, once she got the chance.

Her second dream was the one she'd had hidden in her heart the longest. To have a family. Someone to spend time with. Talk to. Receive comfort and love from. And give the same. That was something she'd never had much of, but longed to lavish on others, and feel in return.

An orphan from the age of four, Poppy couldn't even remember her parents. They were just shadows, flickers in her memories. When she tried to grasp at those flickers, they'd flee. Sometimes, something would move to the forefront, triggering a memory. Like her father's large mustache. The scent of lilac when her mother was near.

Frustratingly, though, there wasn't much Poppy could recall of those early years, and as she'd aged and pretended to be fine, the loss was deep within her. A hollow that couldn't be filled. Even here at the boarding house, she seemed to be the exception. Others talked of family, had pictures of them to show or put in a frame. She had none.

All Poppy had was the aunt she'd lived with, until she was nine and the woman had passed away, and then the aunt's friend, who'd taken care of her until she was thirteen. Two days after her birthday, there had been the opportunity to be a live-in nursery maid, and Poppy took that eagerly, anxious to escape being sent to an orphanage when her aunt's friend decided she no longer wished to raise Poppy. It was better, she decided, to forge her own path than be shuffled to yet another place that bore the reminder she was unloved and unwanted.

Her time in the nursery had been difficult, but there had also been so many moments that Poppy—still a child herself—had enjoyed, especially the playtime, and the care and attention she poured over her young charges, and received in return.

When the children had grown to an age where she was no longer needed, Poppy could have sought working for another family with young children, but she wanted to try something different. It just so happened one day she wandered through town, and spied a Help Wanted sign at the bookstore. At once, she'd pushed her way in and inquired about the job.

For almost two years, she'd worked there six days a week, enjoying her time among the books and the wonderful scent of paper and ink. The owners allowed her to read as much as she wanted, as long as she did the few tasks required of her.

And that's just what she did, turning the pages of books that took her mind on one journey after the next. She'd nearly devoured everything in the store. With her meager pay, she'd bought a book here and there, and well worn pages, especially those with pictures and facts about England and France, fueled her imagination day after day. Since the other boarders knew she loved to read, they'd loan her their volumes as well, and Poppy filled every moment of free time educating herself.

She'd learned so much from her books. That's also why Poppy decided that she wanted to travel and see everything. How could she not, after learning about all of those wonderful things that existed?

But the only way to do that was to have far more money than she did. Or marry a man who traveled. So, as she flipped through the stack of mail, Poppy held her breath, hoping that there was a letter for her from a person who would allow that dream to come true.

As she came to the final piece of mail, Poppy dropped the envelopes back on the table, disappointed. Nothing. She swallowed bitterly, then breathed in deeply, trying to push the sadness away. Perhaps tomorrow. There were a good number of people out there. It might take time for a match to be made. Then, of course, there was the issue of the mail delivery. It had rained so much as of late. That had perhaps delayed things.

She turned to walk away, then noticed an envelope on the floor. It must have blown there when she'd opened the front door. Poppy bent over, picked it up, and had just dropped it on the small table, when she spotted her name.

Miss Poppy Wilson.

Her stomach jolted with excitement. A letter had come! Time seemed to slow as Poppy snatched up the letter and stared at it. Once she was sure that it was, indeed, for her, she carefully opened the envelope and pulled out the letter inside with trembling fingers. Two smaller pieces of paper fell out, and Poppy realized they were train tickets.

"My goodness," Poppy whispered as she looked at them, staggering over to the stairs that led to the second story. She sat on the next to last step and then read the letter.

After a moment, Poppy rubbed her eyes in disbelief. She read the letter twice more, then pressed a hand to her spinning stomach.

A match. They had found a match for her. And not just any! But a man with two little girls, and who *traveled*. This truly was going to be the most perfect thing ever. It was just what she wanted. Thank goodness her friend had come into the shop that day!

It took almost everything in her not to childishly skip back to her room, squealing and giggling with excitement. Calmly, Poppy walked up the stairs and unlocked her door.

But once there, Poppy grinned widely, pulled out her suitcase, and started to pack. The ticket said she left in two days. That wasn't much time at all. She had to make a list of all there was to do.

First would be to let the bookstore owners know. Really, the letter couldn't have come at a better time! Just that morning, they'd apologized profusely, but told her they were closing the shop to retire, and she had a week to find somewhere else to go. This letter would not only rectify her new and sudden financial situation, but also perhaps ease the owners' consciences.

Poppy looked at the tickets once more, slowly running her finger along the words. Soon, she'd be on her way. She'd be married. A mother. Everything was about to change. And for the better. She'd been on her own for so long, she couldn't wait to have someone else to share life with, to travel with, and to, hopefully, love. All it required was a single letter!

Well, and some courage, but she had plenty of that. It was just a little bit scary, the idea of traveling to meet someone she'd never met, and to become his wife, but she knew it happened every day. And she also had the option to leave before they wed, if she didn't like him.

But he traveled! Had children who needed *her*! It was a ready-made family, and just what she wanted. It was a dream come true, and a chance to have all that felt missing from her life.

Poppy spun around the room and closed her eyes for a moment, wondering what her soon-to-be husband would look like. Tall and dark? Muscular and blond? Perhaps he was short, with red hair like her own. And what of the little girls? The letter neglected to mention their ages, but little girls were delightful, and always so imaginative.

She let her mind drift to the usual activities the children she'd minded before enjoyed, and imagined doing all of the things these little girls must love doing, like tea parties, long walks in gardens, reading or acting out stories, making fairy houses with twigs and leaves and flowers.

And travel, of course. They must also travel a good deal. How darling they must look in matching travel suits. She'd have to be sure to get one right away as well. As she'd never traveled before, she didn't own one.

Poppy returned to her packing, unable to stop thinking about the picture-perfect life that she'd been invited into. As she sat on her suitcase and wriggled about trying to close it, her heart felt about to burst with all of the joy within her.

Chapter 3

South Falls, Kansas

Preston Parker fastened his briefcase, and then grabbed his black suit jacket off the back of his chair. As he thrust his arms through the sleeves, a sudden thought sprang to mind.

"Ticket, where did I put that ticket?" he muttered, first checking the outside pockets of the jacket and then the inside. Nothing.

But as his hand reached into the left breast pocket, a wriggling mass jumped into his hand, then over it. Preston stood, watching as a rather warty toad hopped across his study and sprang onto the windowsill, where it let itself out through the cracked window. He closed his eyes for the briefest of moments, let out a deep sigh, and then resumed the search for his tickets.

A moment later, finding them in the very last pocket, of course, he slipped into his freshly shined shoes the housekeeper left outside the door. And watched as white shaving foam rose up from the tops.

"This is absolutely the last straw," Preston muttered.

He inhaled deeply, pulled his feet from the mess, and retrieved a different pair of socks and shoes before storming out of his study. "Anna, Aria," he called. "I know you are behind this. Show yourselves."

No twin terrors appeared, but Preston could hear their giggles. He headed toward them. "This isn't the least bit funny, nor ladylike," he said, stalking over to the large cream-colored floor to ceiling curtains and yanking them back. "It also isn't fair to me or to my shoes."

The twins, both with blonde curls, blue eyes, and impish expressions, threw themselves at him, wrapping their arms about his middle.

"Don't leave us, Uncle Preston," Anna begged, giving him her best sweet expression as she stared up at him. "Please."

"I've got to go, little duck," he told her, feeling a pang of guilt. "But I'll be back."

"I don't like it when you leave," Aria cried, burying her face in his stomach. "What if you don't come back?"

The words stilled him. He thought about that each and every time he left them. And, seeing as they'd lost their parents three years before, he didn't wonder that the eight-year-olds feared he'd leave as well. Still, he had to work. He must do his job.

Though their deceased parents had provided some for the girls in their estate, it was his job that now provided for them, and would see they had a future without fear of financial insecurity. After all, one day they would grow up, and want additional education or a family of their own, and he needed to be sure they had just that, supporting them however he could.

"I'll be back, lamb," he told Aria, trying to soothe her as he squeezed both twins tightly. "But playing tricks on me isn't going to make me stay. It's just going to make me late and unhappy so I leave without a good memory."

"Girls, you know your uncle is a busy man," the housekeeper, Mrs. Fraser, scolded as she bustled into the hallway. "Off you go. I'll get the shoes cleaned, sir."

"Thank you." Preston sighed. "I apologize for the mess."

"You've nothing to apologize for," the housekeeper said.

The twins hugged him once more, then ran off, presumably to plot their next hijinks. If things continued, Preston was sure he'd be gray before he was twenty-eight in a few months. He headed down the stairs of the large house, the housekeeper right behind him.

"What a start to the day. However, I've some good news for you," he told the housekeeper. "The woman from the nanny agency should arrive within the week. I applied for a governess, as the girls are a bit too old for a nanny now. It's my hope that will significantly lighten your load, but also give the girls some stability. Perhaps encourage them to mind their manners better."

As the housekeeper started to protest, Preston added, "You've done the best you can, I know you have, but you can't be housekeeper, educator, and everything else for the girls. It's my fault for delaying so long. I'm sorry for that."

"You have no need to blame yourself," the housekeeper said. "No one does more than you. I'm sure whoever she is will be very experienced." Mrs. Fraser added, "I've heard wonderful things about the Gardner Nanny Agency."

"As have I," he said, pulling open the front door and stepping onto the porch. "Start her right away. I'll be back in two weeks, I hope."

"Don't worry about us," Mrs. Fraser called as he hurried toward the train station, briefcase tucked under his arm.

But he would. He always did. Not just because his job took him away from the girls, who so obviously needed his attention. But also because he hadn't ever planned to be a father. He hadn't ever planned to marry. Preston enjoyed his job. He found a good deal of satisfaction in it. However, there was a dangerous aspect to it as well, which was why he'd never pursued a woman nor the thought of one.

When you didn't know if you'd come home at the end of the day, it made you think twice about all you did.

If only his brother had.

Preston didn't fault his brother for falling head over heels for a woman and having the twins a year later. But he did, at times, feel upset that he, who knew nothing about children, had been the one to take over their care. They were family, and of course he'd do all he could, but his brother's will had been very specific. No boarding school for the twins. They were to be educated at home.

It made things difficult. Especially as Paul had known very well what he did. His brother had done it too. But there was nothing to be done about the situation. It was what it was. Preston had done his best for three years. However, it had gotten to the point he needed help. He had to have a woman there, helping the twins grow into the lovely young women they would be one day. There were so many things only a woman could teach young girls, and they would learn it best from a governess, not an overworked housekeeper.

There was another reason why it was so important to have a governess. He needed to have someone there to care for them if the worst happened, and something... No. He wouldn't think about that.

Thankfully, there was a young woman on the way to take care of everything related to the girls, and his days of worry would end.

Chapter 4

The world had sped by at a rate Poppy had never imagined she'd see. Sometimes, it was almost as though the trees they passed were little more than green blurs. She had no idea that a train could travel so quickly. It was both exciting and strange.

Poppy didn't want to sleep in case she missed something. She saw towns fly past, wide open plains that seemed to go on forever, and endless stretches of bright blue sky. They passed a forest, and Poppy had shivered, imagining train robbers hiding in the dense shrubbery. A moment later as they whooshed past, she saw a field of wheat, and another of corn, the stalks stretching up to meet the clouds.

Though the benches on the train were quite hard, and it was impossible to get completely comfortable, Poppy didn't let that bother her a bit. She was only going to be on the train for a day, but, and perhaps most importantly, she was *traveling*. Seeing things. Going places. And it was just the start.

She wondered about the first place she'd travel to with her new husband. Did he ever go to Europe? She'd always wanted to go there. But, really, she'd be happy with anywhere. Maybe they'd go on a short wedding trip. As she'd never gone anywhere or done much of anything, it didn't matter to her what they did. Just as long as it was something.

The train pulled into a station for a short stop, and Poppy joined the rush of people getting off to buy something to eat and drink. She'd learned that was allowed, as the train would stop for ten minutes each time it took on new passengers or said farewell to others. Anxious not to be left behind, she dashed over to the first person she saw selling food, a woman perhaps in her forties, with hand pies both sweet and savory. She bought two of each, along with a large jar of water, and scurried back on board the train, dropping her heavy suitcase at her feet.

Fortunately, she'd been able to sit alone the majority of the journey. Poppy wasn't sure if she'd like sharing the bench seat and feeling obligated to talk with a stranger. While most everyone looked like an average sort of person, a few of the men appeared rather rough, and it made her nervous. She'd be glad when they arrived.

The next three hours, Poppy read and stared through the window. They zipped past cattle, farmhouses, horses, and endless fences.

"South Falls," the conductor called out as he walked the aisles.

"Oh! That's me," Poppy gasped, and readied herself to leave the train.

As before, a crowd of people dashed off and more took their places on the platform. Clutching her suitcase on the platform, Poppy stood looking about, uncertain as to where she was to go.

Though she'd read the letter a few times on the train, there hadn't been anything in it about what to do once she arrived, or where to go. She only knew the name of the man she was to marry. All other details were missing.

Poppy waited uncomfortably. After a few moments, she stood alone on the platform, and the anxious feeling grew. There wasn't anyone from the town looking for a passenger. A slightly nervous feeling filled her. Now that she was here, where was she to go?

"Looking for someone, miss?" an older man dressed in a stationmaster's clothing asked.

"Yes," Poppy said, pulling the letter she'd gotten with her husband-to-be's name. "I thought I'd be met, but...I guess not. Would you know where Mr. Preston Parker lives? He's expecting me."

"Sure do," he told her. "You can walk there. Only take a few minutes." He pointed down the road. "Go straight. Turn right at the school, down the road a ways, left at the big tree with a swing on it, and it's the white house with a large porch and garden."

Poppy bit her lip and nodded. "Thank you," she said, feeling very nervous. It sounded simple enough, but what if she went to the wrong house?

"There's four rocking chairs on the front porch," the man added. "Two big, two small. You'll be all right."

She nodded again and set off the way he pointed before she forgot the directions he'd told her. Poppy was many things, she'd agree. Capable, clever, patient, just to name a few. But one thing she wasn't, was naturally oriented when it came to getting from one place to the next. Though she had been given many gifts and talents, a sense of direction was not one of them. She prayed that this wasn't the time it failed her.

Thankfully, the old man was right, and it wasn't difficult to find the house. It was rather large, the biggest one that she'd passed, and she wondered how many rooms were inside. There must have been at least a dozen. Timidly, she climbed the front steps and knocked.

As she waited, Poppy tried not to feel more nervous than she was. First impressions were everything. She knew that. Her hands ran along her skirt. She hoped she wasn't too dusty. Since it hadn't been a terribly long journey, she couldn't look too bad. But now, Poppy was regretting not having a chance to glance in a mirror.

The door flung open just then, and two little girls stared at her before they slammed the door in her face.

Poppy blinked. "Ummm," she said, then hurriedly moved to the window to catch sight of her reflection. Had something about her frightened them? Just as she'd moved, the door opened again, and an older woman stood there.

"Ah, hello," Poppy said, quickly turning to her. "I'm Poppy Wilson."

The woman's face lit up. "From the agency?"

"Yes," Poppy answered, feeling instantly a thousand times better. She *was* wanted! They *had* been expecting her! No one waiting for her at the station was likely an oversight. "That's right."

"Come in, come in," the woman said, grabbing Poppy's suitcase. "I'm sorry about the girls. I'm so glad you are here. We've needed a governess for a long time. I'm so glad Mr. Parker sent away for one at last."

"I'm happy to—wait. Did you say a governess?" Poppy asked, feeling confused.

The older woman must not have heard her, though, as she led her through the front foyer. The girls, twins,

Poppy saw now, ran past, one chasing the other and both shrieking.

"Let me show you to your room," the other woman shouted. "I'm Mrs. Fraser. The housekeeper."

"It's a pleasure to meet you," Poppy said, raising her voice as well, as the children raced back past the bottom of the stairs, still shrieking, only it looked like they'd switched who was chasing who.

As they got to the second floor, the noise diminished, and Poppy's ears stopped ringing.

"I'm sorry, the girls can be a handful," Mrs. Fraser said. "And it doesn't help they miss their uncle. He should be home in a few days, and they'll somewhat calm down."

"I hate to broach the subject," Poppy said, as she followed the housekeeper into a bedroom she'd opened the door to. "But you said governess. I think there may be a mistake. I wasn't sent here to be a governess."

"But you said you were Poppy Wilson," the housekeeper said, turning to her and raising her eyebrows in surprise. "And Mr. Parker said a Poppy Wilson was coming from the Garden something or other Agency to be a governess."

Poppy nervously twisted her fingers. "I am Poppy Wilson. Yes. And the Garden Belles Mail-Order Brides Agency sent me." Her voice sounded small, even to her ears. "They are a matchmaking agency. It sounds like there's been some sort of a mistake. I thought I was to marry a man with children. Not be a governess for a man with children."

"Oh dear." Mrs. Fraser put her hands on her hips. "Well, I don't know. Goodness. What a mix-up indeed." She sighed and looked sympathetic. "I'm afraid I don't know anything about that. But Mr. Parker will be back soon. Will you consider staying here until then and helping me with the girls? I'm sure he will straighten everything out once he arrives."

The woman's tone was near pleading, and her face matched. It only took Poppy a moment to decide. After all, what else could she do? She'd come all this way, and it would take time to contact the Garden Belles, if this was a mistake.

"Of course," Poppy said. "I'd be happy to. Whichever capacity I'm here for, the girls are to be in part my responsibility. I'm sure Mr. Parker and I will quickly sort things out once he returns, and do whatever is best for all involved."

Mrs. Fraser's face relaxed, and she reached out to squeeze Poppy's hands. "Thank you, dear. Now, you've just gotten here, so don't plan to do anything but freshen up and relax. Tomorrow is soon enough to meet the twins and begin."

Poppy nodded, but when the other woman left, her nerves returned full force. A governess? That wasn't what she'd agreed to at all! But Poppy was determined to make the best of the situation, until Preston arrived and things were set straight. They surely would be, wouldn't they?

As she started to unpack, Poppy nodded to herself. Yes, things would be fixed as soon as he arrived. The housekeeper must have things quite wrong. She was there to be married, not be household staff.

Chapter 5

Rubbing at his eyes, Preston looked once more at the pile of papers before him. It felt like he'd been staring at it for hours. Maybe he had. Time was blending together, as it often did when he was working.

Yawning, he picked up papers and spread them before him on the desk. Maybe if he did that, something would catch his eye. There had to be something he was missing. But what was it? The sooner he figured it out and found the problem, the sooner he could get home.

Home. He hoped Anna and Aria were doing well, and not causing too much trouble for Mrs. Fraser. The woman was as patient as she could be, but even a saint would eventually lose their temper because they wanted attention. Missed having someone dote on them completely like their mother had done. But that didn't make it any easier for him. Just because you knew something didn't mean you could do anything about it.

Stretching his back with a groan, he looked back over the papers, muttering to himself. "It doesn't make sense. None of this is adding up."

Preston dropped his head into his hands for a moment. His eyes were bleary. After returning to the hotel just after two in the morning, Preston had gotten a few hours of sleep, gone back to the railroad until three in the afternoon, and when he returned to the hotel, sat at this desk staring at these papers for nearly four hours, trying to puzzle out an answer to help the railroad. He had to figure this out. It was not only his job, but people depended on him.

That wasn't the entirety of it, either. Not just people, but people's lives also depended on him.

His stomach growled with growing urgency, and the gnawing ache became uncomfortable. He'd missed lunch. But this was more important.

Preston hunched over the desk again, shuffling the papers. Perhaps if he put them in a different order? His stomach protested again. Maybe the problem was that he was too tired to concentrate. Perhaps a bite would restore him and help him find that missing link.

He stood, deciding to go to the hotel restaurant for some dinner and a short break, when there was a knock at the hotel room door. He tensed. "Who is it?" he called, reaching for his jacket.

"Letter for you, Mr. Parker," Jimmy, the teenage boy who did a bit of everything at the hotel, called out from the hallway.

Preston opened the door a crack, then wider, when he saw the boy. He slipped Jimmy some coins and then accepted the letter. It was from home. He frowned, tapping it in his hand. Mrs. Fraser didn't usually write. He hoped nothing was wrong. If there was something urgent, she knew what to do. So, what was this?

He opened it, and pulled out the letter, dropping the envelope on the room's desk.

Mr. Parker,

All is well, and I apologize for any concern you experienced at my letter's arrival. I wanted to let you know that the governess you'd told me about, Miss Poppy Wilson, has arrived. However, there might be a misunderstanding I wanted you to be aware of before you came home.

The young woman claims she was sent from a mail-order bride agency. She showed me the letter she received from them, and it appears that it is true. She traveled an entire day by train to get here. Obviously, there has been some sort of mix-up. Thankfully, she has agreed to mind the children—and she's doing a wonderful job of it—until you return.

But, for the sake of both your future and the young woman's, not to mention that of the twins, you'll want to see if you can figure out what's happened. Perhaps the letter you were sent will give you a clue.

Safe travels,

Mrs. Fraser

Preston's eyebrows were raised so high, they nearly touched his blond hair, of that he was sure. On one hand, it was quite good the governess had arrived. On the other, where had she gotten the idea that she was sent by a mail-order bride agency? He was quite sure he'd addressed the letter to the Gardner Nanny Agency.

Had his letter been delivered to the wrong place? But if it had, why hadn't they returned it? Or sent it on to the correct one? He'd received a reply, and with this very young woman's name.

He rubbed at his forehead. There was nothing he could do right now, and he didn't have the letter he'd been sent with him, but Preston knew he would be sorting this out the moment he got home. He had no idea where the woman had gotten the impression he was seeking a wife—he was not.

He was not getting married, and didn't need a governess with *ideas*. That would just lead to problems for him, for the twins, and for the woman, if she had her heart set on something she was not going to get.

He shoved the letter into the envelope and put it in his briefcase. He was weary, but grateful for his frustration to have turned from work problems to those of the governess, which proved to be a pleasant distraction. Perhaps it would even allow his mind the time it needed to rest and see his work situation with fresh eyes. That would be helpful.

Preston went down the hallway and to the hotel stairs. They led him to a modest lobby, where the restaurant was tucked in the corner. "Table for one," he said after he was greeted, and walked past women having tea, a few men talking business, and several couples.

After browsing the menu, Preston ordered a bowl of chowder with some rolls. While he waited for his food, he tried not to stare or eavesdrop, but one of the couples was having an animated conversation, and not even trying to be quiet.

"But you are to marry me!" the woman protested, her blonde curls bouncing. "I left that dusty town, and that rancher, to come here! I was promised a life of luxury, and that's just what I want. If I'd wanted to be poor, I'd have married Joseph as his mail-order bride."

"Bess," the man sighed. "I've given you all you've asked. But a new dress a week? Isn't that excessive? Can't we do one a month? Or less?"

The woman continued to protest and pout, and Preston was glad when his meal arrived, so he could focus on that. Women were needy. Always wanting more. At least, that had been his experience. Maybe it wasn't true about all women, but the ones who had found their way into his life had been. They'd also always had some sort of ulterior motive. Was that just who he attracted?

There had been Nina, who wanted a ring on her finger on their second date. He later found out that was because she was expecting in five months. Then, there was Carla, who he had been fond of, but she'd let slip one day she wasn't looking to settle, just for a man to provide for her. And she already had two others in addition to him.

Janice...well, he wasn't going to even think about her. He'd thought she was the one, but again, she'd wanted something else. And she'd almost gotten it too, until the police caught her, with his watch, a pile of cash from his study, and his grandmother's ruby brooch.

Then the twins came along, and Preston knew that there wasn't room for him to make a mistake in a relationship. The girls deserved the best. He'd sworn to give it to them, and that's what he planned to do. And that meant none of the women who seemed to find him. So, that's why this woman he'd hired to become a governess was simply going to stay as such. A governess. Nothing more. If he kept her on. She might be more trouble than she was worth.

It didn't matter that love was out there, he thought to himself as he glanced toward another couple, their heads close, their hands touching, and oblivious to the world around them. It would simply be too dangerous to invite someone new into his home. Both for him, and for the twins.

Chapter 6

The first day there at the Parker residence was almost enough to make Poppy think twice about hoping to become Mrs. Parker. Her first morning, she'd joined the twins and the housekeeper for breakfast.

The girls had generally acted naughty. But Poppy had soldiered through it, ignoring most of their antics, without showing how distressed she was. Not about how they'd "accidently" dropped globs of butter and jam on her dress when leaning over or how salty her tea was when they'd "helped" dump sugar in.

After breakfast, she watched the twins through the window as they sat outside with their small dolls, having a tea party with leaves.

The housekeeper walked up next to her and said, "They can be good girls. I promise you that. Just...it's been hard on them. Especially for the last year, as Mr. Parker has been away so much."

"Have they had a governess or a nanny before?" Poppy asked, though in truth she was wondering how many they'd run through.

"No, it's always been Mr. Parker and me. But my old bones can't keep doing it and running the household," the housekeeper explained.

Poppy had only nodded, but spent the rest of the day observing the twins, not giving in to the frustration or the upset she felt at how chaotic the girls were. If they weren't playing tricks, they were running and screaming, their hair ribbons loose, their hands and faces dirty, and their dresses and shoes dusty.

To top things off, it appeared she was to teach them as well. It was a far cry from what she'd imagined when she was traveling here. Poppy let herself entertain the idea of defeat and seeking employment or a husband elsewhere, but refused to give in. Something told her that's what the girls expected. She would not let that happen. There was no reason that they couldn't be well behaved, and she was going to see to it.

On her second day, Poppy was ready to stop at least some of the pranks before they started. She drank her tea plain, buttered and jammed the girls' breakfast biscuits, and sat them up at their own table, with their dolls in chairs also, to have a breakfast tea party. When she noticed the girls seemed to enjoy that, she decided to do something similar for lunch, and created a small picnic for herself and the girls a few hours later.

That had gone over surprisingly well. She'd helped the girls to wash their faces and hands, and change into clean dresses, explaining that was part of the fun, dressing up as though it were a real party. There, they'd had a picnic together in the garden, and Poppy had brought outside both a book she'd found in the house and a game she made the night before.

It was a simple matching game, with identical images on squares of paper she'd quickly drawn, but the girls enjoyed testing their memories, and "besting" her and each other as they turned the pieces over, two at a time.

Shadows were starting to fall by the time the girls were losing interest in the game. Poppy noticed that the entire time they'd been outside, and she'd engaged with them, they'd been angels. Their behavior must be to get attention, she surmised. But, why? Many children were content playing on their own for a while.

She wondered if there was something that made them fearful of being alone. It wouldn't surprise her. She'd felt that way as a girl after losing her mother. Only, she didn't have the comfort of a sibling, instead having an aunt who didn't seem to care to ease young Poppy's fears.

Perhaps they were simply bored, and lacked the manners they needed because they were left to their own devices too often. She wasn't sure, but planned to continue to observe the girls and see if she could find out.

"Have you ever built houses for your dolls?" Poppy asked, as she put the picnic items into the basket Mrs. Fraser had loaned them.

"No, but that sounds fun. How do we do that?" Anna asked.

"I will show you tomorrow, after lunch," Poppy promised. "Perhaps we can have our lunch outside again, and then we will have a nice blanket to build upon."

"Why not now?" Aria asked. "Or in the morning?"

"Because right now," Poppy said, "we are going to go inside and make cookies. And in the morning, after breakfast, we will take a walk."

The twins exchanged looks. "I always wanted to make cookies," Anna said.

"But Mrs. Fraser won't let us in the kitchen," Aria finished.

"I'm sure she will change her mind," Poppy said, standing and brushing off her dress. "We just need to promise to clean up afterward, so we don't make more of a mess for her. And," she added sternly, "you must follow directions. Do you know what will happen if you play a trick while in the kitchen?"

"You'll get mad?" Anna asked.

"You'll tell Uncle?" Aria asked. She laughed then. "He won't do anything."

Poppy shook her head. "The kitchen is full of dangerous things, like a hot stove and knives. Someone could get very hurt. And if you played a trick and switched the ingredients around, someone could get very sick, and the hard work you put into making those cookies would be wasted. As would the cost of the ingredients. That would be terrible and then no one could enjoy them, and you wouldn't be allowed to make more."

The girls were quiet, then Aria said quietly, "We didn't know."

"You mean," Poppy corrected, "you didn't think about the consequences of your actions. Everything we do has a result. Some are good, some bad. But right now, you've both been so lovely today, and Mrs. Fraser has worked so hard, I think our consequence should be a treat for us all."

The girls eagerly followed Poppy to the kitchen, where they washed up, tied large aprons around themselves, and made sugar cookies. The kitchen got a little messy, as to be expected, but the three had a wonderful time. Poppy taught them to create shapes from the dough, and after dinner, the twins, Poppy, and Mrs. Fraser declared them the finest cookies they'd ever eaten.

"Can we save some back for Uncle Preston?" Anna asked.

"We can try," Poppy agreed. "If they start to spoil or get hard before he's home, we will simply have to eat them and make some new ones."

"Does that mean you'll stay for a while?" Aria asked.

Poppy wasn't sure how to answer. "I...I don't know," she finally said. "You see, I came here not realizing that your uncle thought I was coming to be a governess."

"What's wrong with being a governess?" Anna asked.

"Nothing," Poppy said. "I worked in a nursery for a long time. But, I'm older now. I want..." She didn't finish. She couldn't. Heat pricked at her eyes.

"What do you want?" Aria asked.

"I want to travel," Poppy finally answered, standing to clear away the plates. "And to have a family of my own."

"We want that too," Anna whispered. "The family part. That's why you should stay. We'd like you in our family."

Poppy stood between their chairs, and put an arm around each of the girls. She drew in a deep breath, unsure how to help the girls or herself, and asked, "How about a bedtime story once you have washed and gotten ready for bed?"

The twins quickly agreed, and soon Poppy found herself in their room, reading the girls one of their favorite stories. When their eyes drooped, and their breathing became steady, she tiptoed out of the room and into her own, where she changed into her nightdress and got into bed.

She was finding her position here a little confusing. She liked the girls, and wanted to help them. It astonished her how quickly she'd grown to love them, and them her. Inside of each of them, she could see the potential that they had to be young ladies who grew into clever young women. But, that wasn't entirely why she'd come here. And if the chance for marriage wasn't on the horizon, then Poppy wasn't sure she wanted to stay. It would be a disservice to herself, and as she had no one to look out for her best interests, she must do it herself.

She'd heard other nannies and governesses complain. They spent their years caring for others, and were left alone with nothing to show for it. Poppy didn't want that to be her. Not when there was so much out there she longed to see, and that special someone she wanted to have a family with.

If Preston wasn't to be him, then she'd have to keep looking. That man was out there, and now that she'd gotten a taste of a family, she wanted it even more.

Her earlier tears burned again, but Poppy was determined not to cry. Not to let herself be that fearful girl, who felt unloved and unwanted. She could figure this out. She just had to wait until Mr. Parker returned.

Just then, she heard a sound, and her door eased open. Poppy sat up in surprise as two little figures scampered over. "Girls," she said. "Did you have a bad dream?"

Anna and Aria stood there quietly. Poppy lit the lantern next to her bed, and saw their sweet faces wet with tears. "Goodness," she said, pulling back the bedclothes. "Come here. Tell me what's wrong."

The girls climbed in the bed, one on each side of her. Poppy wrapped her arms around them again. "Now then," she said, "tell me what has happened."

"We don't want you to go," Aria whispered.

"We will be good and stop playing tricks," Anna hiccupped, "if you can stay."

"My dears, that is not entirely up to me," Poppy said. "I will tell you the whole truth. You see, I thought I was coming here to marry your uncle. Not be the governess for his nieces."

"You mean..." Anna stared at her in shock.

"We could have a mama again?" Aria finished. "Or, at least, an aunt?"

"I don't know," Poppy said with a sigh. "That's not really up to me. It appears there was a misunderstanding. I was told we would be married, and your uncle, I think, was told he was getting a governess. Those are two very different things, and I can't promise that your uncle will want me to marry him."

"I think he should," Anna said firmly, crossing her arms over her chest.

"Is that so?" Poppy teased. "Because you want me to stay?"

"That," Aria agreed, "and because we want Uncle Preston to be happy. He never smiles anymore. I bet you could make him smile."

Poppy wondered about that curious statement, as the girls snuggled into the bed, talking with each other. He never smiled? Was that because of life's worries? The twins' behavior? Or was it something else she had no chance of helping with or overcoming, like an unrequited love?

Chapter 7

Preston wearily stepped off the train and onto the platform. It wasn't the journey that had been tiring, but his work. He'd hardly slept, what with being on near edge with his men trying to stop the—

"Mr. Parker!"

He paused mid-step and turned, then nodded at the stationmaster. "Mr. Peters," he greeted, wondering what the man wanted.

"Got a right pretty woman at your place," the man said, rocking back on his heels.

"A governess for my nieces," Preston answered, giving a tight smile. He'd quite forgotten about her for a few moments. Now that she was brought to mind, the stress filling him magnified.

"Sure, sure," the man laughed, and walked away.

Preston fought back a growl, and hurried toward his home. What had the man been insinuating? Unless...unless he'd said that because the woman wasn't being a very good governess. Had the girls been causing so much trouble the whole town knew of it?

His heart sank, and he mentally steeled himself for the onslaught that was about to happen the moment he opened the house door. The twins would have some sort of a prank. The only question was, how messy or disastrous would it be?

That was two questions, wasn't it? Perhaps there should be a third. Would the young woman who'd arrived still be there, or would they have sent her running?

The house was up ahead, and Preston neared it, trying to force his legs to move. They felt heavy, weighted by his reluctance to see what had happened in his absence. He was about to step onto the porch when he heard voices coming from the garden. It sounded like the twins.

Quietly, he set his belongings down and stepped toward the garden gate. What he saw halted him.

Anna and Aria were intently building something. He wasn't sure what, but they were completely enraptured by it. The small China dolls he'd gotten them for birthdays and Christmas were nearby, along with a scattering of plates with cookies on them. They were so focused on their activity, they didn't see him, and Preston took a moment to watch, enjoying seeing his nieces' peaceful expressions.

Then, he saw her. A woman with light red hair, whose lovely face made his heart do a funny little flip. She offered Anna a purple flower, and asked, "What of this one?"

"That will do very nicely," his niece agreed. "Aria, your dolls simply must come and visit mine for tea."

"Oh yes," Aria chirped, marching one of her dolls closer. "What a lovely home you've built, Anna."

Preston stood, completely captivated by the sight. He couldn't get over the fact his nieces looked so happy. So content. So calm. His eyes flicked to the woman he assumed was the governess and the one responsible for this miraculous moment.

As if she sensed someone looking at her, the woman glanced his way, and gave a little gasp as she startled. The twins followed her gaze, and then jumped up excitedly.

"Uncle Preston!" Anna squealed as she rushed to the gate. "Come look at my house."

"Look at mine too," Aria pleaded, grabbing his hand and tugging him into the garden.

"Look," Anna said, pointing to a teacup where clover, both the flowers and the leaves, lay heaped in it. "We were just about to have a tea party with this clover soup we made."

"It looks wonderful," Preston told her with a smile, feeling much better than he had a short time ago. Then he turned his attention to the woman before him. "Hello. Miss Wilson?"

"Poppy," Aria corrected him. "We call her Poppy."

"Poppy," Preston said, liking the way her name felt on his tongue. He realized then that he shouldn't be so familiar. Not when a larger issue hung over them. The problem of her thinking she'd come to marry him.

"Ah, girls," he said, turning his attention temporarily to the twins, "I'd like to speak with Miss Wilson—Poppy—for a few moments."

"About seeing if she'll stay?" Anna asked, her face hopeful.

"Girls, why don't you see if there are some of the cookies that you made left, and get those and a drink for your uncle? I'm sure he's tired after traveling all day," Poppy said. "And I know he'd love to taste what you made. You could set them out for him."

Aria made a face, but stood up. "We miss all the good stuff."

"Don't forget to wash first," Poppy called as they skipped through the gate.

Preston watched in surprise as his nieces obeyed. This woman must have some way about her. They had never listened so well for him.

When he returned his attention to the governess, she was staring at him, waiting patiently with her hands folded in front of her. No, that wasn't quite right. Her hands were clasped, because she was trying not to fidget in worry. Preston hated that he made her feel that way.

"Preston Parker," he said, offering his hand suddenly. He wasn't sure why he'd done that, as it was obvious she knew who he was.

But as her soft hand reached for his, and he marveled at how small and how nice it felt, Preston worried he was going to be in trouble. When their eyes locked, and he found himself nearly lost in her expressive face, he knew it for certain.

Miss Poppy Wilson was going to either be a force to be reckoned with or his undoing.

It didn't matter, though. What he had to say needed to be said. Even if every inch of him was fighting for him to be quiet or change his mind. She could only stay as the governess.

But if she did, he had a terrible feeling he might regret it.

Chapter 8

Poppy waited, her stomach a terrible mass of nerves all jangling around and making her feel as though she was going to be sick. She tried to tell herself not to feel that way. That she was an adult, and in the right. She had the letter as proof she was meant to be here, meant to be his wife. But none of that mattered if he didn't want her there or in that capacity.

So, instead of speaking, she tried to breathe calmly, count backward for as long as it took, press her hands together tightly to quell any shaking, and wait patiently for him to say whatever it was that would decide her fate here at the Parker residence.

Fortunately, she didn't have to wait too long.

"The housekeeper said there might have been a mistake somewhere," he told her, his amber eyes searching her face. For what, she wasn't sure. "That you arrived from a matchmaking agency, not a nanny agency."

"That's right, Mr. Parker," Poppy said, brushing back her hair as the wind blew a strand into her eyes. "The Garden Belles Mail-Order Brides Agency sent me. I can show you the letter, if you'd like?"

"Garden Belles?" Preston shook his head. "And call me Preston, please. My letter was addressed to the Gardner Nanny Agency. I suppose it was delivered to the wrong place by mistake. And, further, it was opened and answered without anyone realizing what I was looking for. Which is someone to care for the twins."

"A wife can do that," Poppy said, then clapped her hand over her mouth in mortification. Her cheeks flamed in response to her quick tongue. "I mean..."

He sighed, and rubbed at the back of his neck. "I know. And it appears that my nieces not only like you, but obey you. That is a rare thing. However, I'm not intending to get married. In my line of work...well, it doesn't matter. What I need is a governess. I'm sorry. You came out all this way, and stopped whatever you were doing and the life that you had to marry me. I can't make that happen, but I can offer you the job of governess, if you'd like that. The pay will be good, and the girls seem to connect with you. I've never seen that before, with them and Mrs. Fraser."

Poppy was quiet. She took a long moment to go over the words he'd said. He had said he wasn't intending to marry, but did that mean it wasn't a firm no? That he just hadn't planned to, yet? Maybe he was shy. Nervous. Wanted time to get to know a partner before asking her to marry him. Could that be it? Would that be reason enough to stay? The chance at marriage?

Over Preston's shoulder, she could see two small faces pressed against a window, their faces hopeful. She knew that they'd be disappointed if she left. Truthfully, she would be too.

"Well," Poppy finally answered, drawing her attention back to Preston. "I won't lie that I'm disappointed. Your letter was...well, it was the answer to both a prayer and a dream. I've always longed to travel, and I want a family. To have been welcomed into one, as a part of it, not as hired help, was something—is still something—that I want."

"I'm sorry," Preston said, and she could tell from his face that he was. Somehow, that made her feel a little better. "What of your own family? You speak as though you have no one."

Tensing her shoulders, Poppy answered, "That's because I don't. I lost my parents when I was very young. The aunt who took me in died a few years later. I've been on my own since I was thirteen, nearly ten years now, working for one family or place or another."

She laughed then, trying not to sound as hurt and lonely and frightened as she was. The serious situation she found herself in—alone and unwanted in an unfamiliar town—caused her to feel lightheaded and slightly hysterical. It was all she could do to hold that in.

"So, you see, I am an orphan, with no one waiting for me and no one to worry about me. It was why I was so excited. This would have been a chance for great happiness."

Her chest squeezed painfully, and Poppy busied herself with cleaning up the remnants of the dolls' picnic, careful not to disturb the small houses the girls had made. She was sure they'd return to them shortly.

"If it makes you feel any better," Preston said, kneeling next to her to help. "I feel terrible about it. I do."

Poppy gave him a considering look and sat back on her heels. "I know. As do I. It's one of those things that happen in life, and we just can't do much at all, but soldier forth." She was quiet again for a moment, then the words jumped from her lips before she'd even thought them through. "Six months."

"Beg your pardon?" Preston asked.

"I still want to travel, and I want a family. I won't compromise my happiness because of a misunderstanding. I can't. I know what happens to the women who do, and stay in service. But, at the same time, I've grown fond of Anna and Aria in these short days, and I do see how lonely they are. They remind me of myself as a girl, and I understand it takes time to find a governess, and a good one at that.

"So, I'll stay for six months, to give you time to find someone to replace me. In exchange, you'll pay me *very* generous wages, and when I go, pay for my expenses to wherever it is that I head. I will, in the meantime, write the Garden Belles and explain what happened, and that in six months I'll need to find a husband. If they can't find one right away, it's my hope whatever you've paid me will tide me over until I can find a suitable job and affordable lodgings."

"That's more than fair," Preston said.

"I know it is," Poppy said frankly. "And, I don't mean to be rude about my wages, but I don't wish to be taken advantage of. Especially since I sort of already was."

"You'll have them," Preston said. She noted a touch of relief in his voice. "This actually went better than I had hoped. I wasn't sure what to expect. How angry you might get. I wouldn't have blamed you at all for it, though."

"You'll find I'm a very practical individual," Poppy told him. "I've had to be. But," she glanced at the twins, still watching them, "please make sure you find someone loving for the girls. They need that." There was a wistfulness in her voice, she realized. A pain that only one orphan to another could understand.

"I will," Preston told her. He caught her gaze again, and his voice was soft. "They—and you—deserve a happy home."

He stood then, and left the garden, and Poppy wiped away the tear that betrayed her. She did. Yes. But would she ever get it? Would she ever fulfill her dream of a family and travel and love and happiness? Or would she forever be an outsider, looking in and living on the scraps that were thrown to her?

Chapter 9

It was good to be home. After hugging the twins again and retrieving his luggage from where he'd left it outside, Preston carried it to his room and then left for his study to tackle the pile of mail he was sure had come while he was gone.

Walking into his study, he felt a wave of exhaustion come over him. The days had been long while he was gone, and there had been a lot of worry over his job and the twins, and then the shock of the news from Mrs. Fraser that a woman had arrived thinking she was to marry him. He'd been so concerned over what might be happening while he was gone, it had been a tremendous relief to see the girls behaving—enjoying themselves, even—with the new governess.

Who was being extremely kind in staying on for six months while he found a proper governess. He had no doubt that he would, but a twinge or two of guilt filled him at it. He felt terrible that this mistake—not his fault, and not Poppy's—had disrupted her life and led to disappointment.

In truth, he was less inconvenienced than she was. She'd had to leave all she had behind to come out here, expecting a fresh start, a family...

Preston swallowed hard. "Focus. That's not your problem. She did it willingly," he said, trying to ease the guilt.

It didn't work.

Sitting at his desk, he closed his eyes a moment, then opened them, determined to get the guilt and the picture of Poppy's lovely face out of his mind.

After flipping through the stack of letters to see if anything needed his immediate attention or caught his eye, he noticed, to his surprise, that he could see Poppy and the girls outside, in the garden, through one of his windows. He moved to the edge and stood, watching them.

Poppy seemed to be reading aloud while the girls worked together to build a larger structure for their dolls.

It made him decide that they should have a large dollhouse, and he planned to buy them one for Christmas, as it would be too cold to go outside and make one then out of the little things they were using in the garden.

Would the dolls need clothing? Or the house decorated? Perhaps Poppy could—

Poppy wouldn't be there. She'd be gone. A small part of him wondered if he'd made a mistake. If he shouldn't have just married the woman so she'd stay. It seemed to him the twins would be quite fine with that idea. But that wouldn't have been fair to her, or to him. No matter he could give her the things she wanted, that wasn't something he was ready for or wanting. While Preston didn't think he'd be getting any chances at true love, he knew, for a fact, if ever it were to happen, it couldn't be with a stranger.

He sighed, watching as Aria and Anna plopped next to Poppy to look at the book. He never thought he'd see such a thing. How quickly they took to her. And she seemed to love them as well. But it didn't matter. Poppy had to leave and find her own happiness somewhere else. It had to be this way.

Truthfully, he had been surprised at their conversation in the garden. It had gone far differently than he'd imagined. She'd not asked for anything that wasn't fair. She hadn't pressed him or pleaded, tried to get something more from him. There had been no threats, just an open honesty, which he could see in her clear eyes. It had been refreshing. Welcome. And just the sort of thing he appreciated.

A small voice within him whispered that Poppy was just who the girls needed. Preston shook his head. Yes, she was. But, he was a man of his word. He wouldn't keep her from getting what she deserved, not after she'd come all this way and was willing to help him, even though she didn't have to.

He'd send off a letter tonight to the nanny agency, and see who they could match him with. It would be wrong of him to keep Poppy from the life she deserved and the happiness that was surely out there waiting for her because of his selfishness in wanting her there for the girls.

Not to mention there was that strange current that he felt when speaking with her. Something that spoke of a hint of a thing that could be, if he allowed it.

And that whatever it was...he wouldn't. Couldn't.

There was a knock on his door, and he crossed the room to open it. Mrs. Fraser stood there.

"Welcome back," she said, setting down a tray with something light for him to eat. He appreciated it, as he was always famished when he returned home.

"Thank you," he told her. When she stood there, a hesitant expression on her face, but showing no intention of leaving, he asked, "Is there something else?"

"Did you talk to Poppy about staying on?" the housekeeper asked.

"I did," he said with a sigh. "I feel bad. I do. But getting married...it's not in my future. However, she has agreed to stay for six months while I search for a new governess."

"That's kind of her, and I'd have expected nothing less, just from the short time she's been here. Still, it's a shame," Mrs. Fraser said, disappointment on her face and in her tone. "She seems quite good with the girls. They've certainly taken to her."

As could I, Preston thought, and nearly panicked, worrying he'd spoken out loud.

"I hope you can find a good governess," Mrs. Fraser said. "I'm sure that you can, but what I mean is, I hope it's one who can connect with the girls. It's strange how quickly they seemed to bond. After seeing them together, I realize that might be a difficult thing to replicate, but I think it's what the girls need."

"I do as well, and that is my hope too," Preston sighed. "And I'll be doing my best to find such a governess. But I can't force Poppy to stay, and I can't give her what she wants. Especially when she longs to marry and have a family of her own. It wouldn't be right."

"No, it wouldn't be," the housekeeper agreed. "I'm glad you understand that. Many don't. It's a bit different, me having lost my Sam. I had my time with a husband. But I've known many women who spend their whole lives caring for another's family, and in their later years, there's nothing and no one for them. She deserves to experience life while she's young enough and healthy enough to enjoy it. Makes me glad to see a young woman looking after herself, since she has no one else to do so."

Preston was going to agree, but the housekeeper started toward the door before he could answer. "Dinner in an hour," she told him, and closed the door softly behind her.

His legs carried him back to the window before he realized it. There, he watched as Poppy and the twins carried their things into the house from the garden. Anna happened to look up and spotted him. When she waved, Aria did as well.

It was too late to step back, not to be seen, so Preston smiled and returned the wave. Poppy's hands were full, but he noticed she looked at the window, then glanced away quickly, and her cheeks turned the softest pink he'd ever seen as she ducked her head.

For a moment, just the briefest of instances, he felt pleased that he'd done that, eliciting such a genuine reaction from her. Poppy didn't seem to be like any woman he'd ever met. She didn't seem to have some ulterior plan.

And, perhaps it was because of that, his heart wondered what it might be like if he did ever marry a woman like her. One who radiated honesty and practicality and sweetness. One with red hair.

Chapter 10

Two weeks later, Poppy was still getting used to being there at the Parker residence. Overall, she felt quite welcome by Mrs. Fraser and the twins. Preston, she wasn't quite sure about.

At times, she felt a sense of awkwardness when she was around him, and by the way he occasionally stammered, she wondered if he felt the same. Truthfully, the entire situation was awkward. Unusual, too.

Poppy wondered how many other women arrived somewhere for a mail-order marriage and had a mix-up like this one. She hoped not very many, because, for herself, she didn't like the feelings that came with it—a strange mix of sadness and hope he'd reconsider marriage, both feelings that refused to fade. She wouldn't wish those difficult emotions on anyone else.

With a yawn, she rubbed her eyes. It was near midnight, and she should be asleep. Instead, she was pacing her room, trying to burn off some of the restless energy that filled her. It was so strange, too. She should be exhausted.

It had been a long day with the twins and their hijinks. Aria had chased Anna with a garter snake, and then Anna had retaliated by putting a minnow in her tea. Though the tricks hadn't been toward her, they were still trying as she mediated, especially since neither girl had been remorseful.

Still, Poppy supposed there was something to be grateful for, and that was that the pranks had been fewer.

Through her window, Poppy could see the full moon, large and bright. She paused and observed it, her eyes absorbing the beauty and admiring the way it lit the sky. Was that why she couldn't sleep? It was shining in her room? No, that wasn't it. It had to be the upset over the situation she currently found herself in. She was trying to make the best of it, for herself, for the twins, for Mrs. Fraser, and for Preston. But it was hard.

No matter how she tried to tell herself that things would work out, she couldn't help but worry maybe they wouldn't. Maybe she'd always be without a family of her own.

Poppy sat up and reached for her shawl, wrapping it over her nightdress. Perhaps a cup of tea would help her to fall asleep. She was unlikely to run into anyone, but wanted the shawl just in case. It was older, and growing threadbare in places, but it was so soft and the prettiest shade of blue, she wasn't anxious to replace it.

Lighting the small lantern in her room, Poppy picked it up and carefully made her way down the stairs. She pushed open the door from the dining room to the kitchen, expecting to be alone, and was surprised to see another lantern lit and glowing from within.

Also clad in his nightclothes, Preston looked over as she opened the door. "Couldn't sleep?" he asked as casually as if it were midday, and they weren't both dressed for bed.

"Ah, no, I couldn't," Poppy admitted, frozen in the doorway. "I thought I'd make some tea."

"Already steeping," he told her with a grin. "If you don't mind sharing with me? I have enough."

She gave a small laugh. "I don't. Thank you." Poppy walked in and set her lantern down on the kitchen table. She tried not to feel embarrassed at being caught by Preston. He didn't seem the least bit concerned himself, but she wondered if that was because this was his house. For all she knew, he kept late hours.

"Here," he said, bringing over two cups of tea, setting one before her.

"Thank you," Poppy said as she reached for hers.

To her surprise, he didn't sit down, but instead returned to the cabinet. She watched silently as he pulled out two plates, and then removed the glass dome overtop a fresh cake.

"Oh! We shouldn't!" Poppy gasped, as Preston cut into the iced lemon cake.

"We should," Preston said with a wink. "It's best when it's fresh. Don't worry, Mrs. Fraser is used to my ways."

"If you are sure?" Poppy asked, hesitantly.

"I am." He slid a plate and fork in front of her. "What's a midnight tea without a snack?"

"I've never done this," Poppy admitted, "so I wouldn't know." Then she teased, "You seem the expert. I'll just have to take your word for it."

"Yes, you will," he agreed.

They ate a few bites, then he asked, "How are you finding things? The girls, they aren't too much trouble, are they?"

"We are managing," Poppy said. "Every day is easier."

"What did you do before you came? If that's not impolite to ask," Preston said.

"I worked in a bookshop. It was owned by a dear older couple. They had so many wonderful volumes," Poppy said, hearing the wistfulness in her own voice. "I really enjoyed working there."

"I like books too," Preston said. "There are a large number in the house. Feel free to read any of them you like."

"Thank you," Poppy said. "They allowed me to do the same at the shop. I own a few, and I brought them with me. But there..." She shook her head. "It was marvelous. Everything you wanted to read."

"A good book fills many hours," Preston agreed. "Takes you to places and tells you things you never knew existed."

"Yes!" Poppy sat up excitedly. "That's just why I love to read. Books have opened my mind to many new things."

Silence fell on them again, and after a moment, Poppy ventured, "Do you get to travel many places with your work?"

"Not too many," he told her. "Usually just the same few. It gets tiring at times. The same hotels, the same meals."

"I think travel would be fun," Poppy said, then drank from her tea.

"At first, it was. Then it became very lonely," Preston told her. "When I'm gone, it's imperative I concentrate on my work. But sometimes, that's difficult. I worry about Anna and Aria."

"I'll take good care of them," Poppy promised. "You needn't worry."

"I know you will," he told her, but she heard a bit of a sigh in his voice. He ran a hand through his hair. "It's hard, though. When you care for someone. They are often on your mind."

She was quiet. After a moment, she nodded, and said, "Yes, they are."

"Poppy," Preston said, "I am very glad you are here. Thank you for staying. I know the situation isn't ideal, and it's not what you expected. But you didn't have to help me, and I want you to know how grateful I am to you that you are, and how happy I am that you are here."

"I'm glad I'm here too," Poppy said. "I can't think of anywhere else I'd rather be."

And it was true. Of all the things she thought she might do, or hoped she might do in her life, Poppy never imagined drinking tea and eating lemon pound cake after midnight with a man who had been in her thoughts since the moment she'd met him. She also wouldn't trade it for anything. It would become one of those memories that she'd cherish for the rest of her life.

He had no idea how much she cared for him, even though she hardly knew him. Poppy couldn't help but hope that one day, he'd feel the same about her. She couldn't explain it, but deep inside, she knew she belonged here, and she wanted to stay—wanted him—more than anything.

Chapter 11

A month had gone by very quickly. Preston couldn't have been more pleased at the change that had come over the house. The twins were always happy, Mrs. Fraser seemed more at ease, and Poppy...ah, Poppy. He couldn't stop himself from smiling every time he thought about her.

And just as quickly, he made himself stop. Just like he did every other time that ridiculous smile formed. Poppy was there as a governess. Nothing more. He needed to remember that. Not get swept away in the peaceful feeling that filled the house, filled his being at her presence, made his life much richer.

There was a knock on his study door, and Preston called out, "Come in."

The door flung open, and Aria's eager face appeared. "Uncle Preston," she asked, "do you have time to play with us?"

He checked his pocket watch. "I do, lamb," he said. "What game would you like?"

"How about hide and seek?" she asked. "Poppy has agreed to play too."

"Who is counting first?" he asked.

"You are," Aria said, pulling on his arm and leading him up the stairs. "The rules are different. Adults against children. Since this is a team game, you have to hide together and seek together."

"Together?" Preston asked in surprise. He could see Poppy near the top of the stairs, and she also looked taken aback.

"Yes, that's right." Anna put her hands on her hips. "Unless you're scared we'll win?"

"Not at all, duck," he answered. "I'm just not wanting you two to get upset when Poppy and I find you."

"Oh, we won't," both girls said in a singsong voice.

"We'll hide first," Anna said. "Count to one hundred."

"Better run!" Poppy teased. "I'm a fast counter!" She started, "One, two, three..."

The girls ran off, and as soon as Poppy reached one hundred, they started searching for the twins. They weren't in any of their usual hiding places. Poppy and Preston searched each room, peering under furniture, checking behind doors and curtains, and growing exhausted in their search.

A half hour later, Preston plopped down into a chair. "Where are they?" he groaned. "Usually, I can find them easily. They must have learned some new hiding spots."

"I'm starting to wonder if they are even in the house," Poppy said. "We've looked everywhere."

"Let's check the garden then," Preston said, pushing up from the chair.

They walked to the kitchen door, and Preston held it to allow Poppy to go first. She glanced around the lawn, and then walked to the garden fence. "Oh! What's this?" Poppy asked.

Walking toward her, Preston looked over to where she had stopped. There, atop the small table in the garden, were two cups of lemonade, two plates, and a platter with slices of bread. A small pot of honey and another of butter sat next to the platter.

"I don't know," he answered, stepping closer. "Do you think they got tired of playing hide and seek and wanted to do a tea party instead?"

"There are place cards," Poppy said softly, picking up one of the small papers on the plate in front of her. "One for each of us."

He joined her at the table. He could hear giggles coming from near the garden shed. "Come out, you two," he called. "I hear you."

The twins appeared, but ignored him, running over to Poppy. "Do you like our surprise?" they asked her.

"It's a lovely surprise," Poppy said. "It's quite unexpected. Won't you join us?"

"Oh no," Anna said, shaking her head, and backing away.

"We can't. It's not romantic then," Aria giggled.

Both twins ran from the garden and into the house.

Romantic? Preston looked over at Poppy. Her cheeks were flushed, and she looked as though she wasn't sure if she should follow the girls or not. He felt the same. What were those rascals up to?

He glanced toward the house and saw two hopeful faces peering through the window. "Bless their hearts, do they even realize we can see them?" he asked. "That window has permanent nose prints."

"I don't think so," Poppy laughed. Hesitation filled her voice and she asked, "They've gone to so much trouble. Should we?"

Preston walked over, and started to sit, then said, "Wait. Let me get your chair."

He pulled out Poppy's chair, and she sat. They helped themselves to the food and drank the tea, neither of them saying a word. Somehow, though, it was comfortable. Like it had been that night in the kitchen, just the two of them.

Though it had been many weeks, Preston had thought back to that night more times than he should have. He'd also hoped it would happen again, but it hadn't.

Poppy cleared her throat, and Preston gave her his full attention. "I promise," she said, "I am not encouraging them to do this. To...try and get us alone."

"I know," he told her. "They like you a good deal. I don't blame them wanting you to stay. To become their aunt."

Her cheeks turned red, and Preston shifted uncomfortably. Why had he said that? How would he follow it up? He'd made things awkward now, which was not his intent.

"I would like that too," Poppy said, meeting his eyes. "But it is not to be, and I am not wanting you to feel any pressure or as though I am trying to coerce you."

"I appreciate that," Preston mumbled and shoved a bite of bread into his mouth. He felt incredibly uncomfortable now. He wasn't used to this. A woman not trying to get something from him. It made him uncertain about what to do. It was much easier to tell a woman who asked for too much to leave.

How did one tell the woman who seemed to be just right for him to leave? Especially when that wasn't something he wanted.

Poppy is different, he reminded himself. But that made it even more difficult. She was different from every other woman he'd known in such a wonderful way, he was struggling not to think about her each moment of his day.

Over the next week, the twins kept pushing him and Poppy together. If they went for a walk, the twins ran ahead, leaving him and Poppy to walk alone. They went fishing one afternoon, and Anna and Aria insisted they wanted to fish alone, and told him to set up the lunch to help Poppy.

Preston didn't mind, and he was sure Poppy didn't, but it was growing hard. The more time he spent alone or nearly alone with her, the more he liked her. It was dangerous to do such a thing.

But it was almost too late. Preston knew he needed to find another governess, and to find one in a hurry before it was too late and his heart shattered into pieces. He and Poppy couldn't be. The sooner she left, the faster he'd heal. It would be hard to forget her face, her voice, the soft touches she gave on his hand or arm. But he'd have to. She couldn't stay.

He just hoped the girls would be able to forget about her as well because he could tell they loved Poppy every bit as much as he did. Which, was far more than he ever imagined he could.

What was he going to do?

Chapter 12

It had been several months since Poppy had first arrived. As she brushed her hair that morning, braided it into a long tail, and got dressed, she couldn't help but think how much had happened in that time.

The twins still played the occasional prank, both on Poppy and on Preston. However, they were far fewer and milder in nature. In fact, the change in the girls had been remarkable. Mrs. Fraser, on more than one occasion, mentioned how grateful she was, and how she hoped it would last. She had even made sure to say that several times around Preston, giving him a meaningful look. It had been all Poppy could do to not laugh as she had the feeling she knew what that look meant. Goodness knew the girls had begged him to let her stay.

Preston had left several times, usually for just a few days, a week at the most, and had returned from his most recent trip the night before, offering to take the twins and Poppy to enjoy themselves at the fair, which had set up the day before. Poppy was looking forward to going. She hadn't gone on any sort of excursion for quite some time, and she was excited to see what the day might bring.

She also wondered how the search for a new governess was going. Part of her was in no rush to leave, but another part of her was scared of what would happen if she stayed. She'd like to. In fact, she was always a little hopeful that Preston would tell her that he'd called off the search for a governess, and he only wanted her. As his wife.

Poppy sighed as she let that thought drift through her mind. Preston. He was...complicated. He seemed serious. Kind to his nieces, thoughtful, but always stoic, as though a great weight were on him. She wondered what it was, and if she could help.

Once, she'd broached the subject to Mrs. Fraser, who simply shook her head and said, "He's always been that way. He bears a great responsibility both with his job and in caring for the twins."

No more was said, and Poppy wondered just what aspect of his job was so difficult. Truthfully, she knew nothing more than what the twins told her, that he worked for the railroad, as had their father. She knew he wasn't a manual laborer, so she assumed he was a businessman of some sort.

Did he do accounting? Draw the plans for new tracks? Maybe he bought the land for the railway company to expand their tracks. She wasn't sure. She didn't even know the railway company's name.

Poppy would have asked more questions, but really, it wouldn't have been appropriate. Preston didn't intend to marry her, and she knew that she was hired help right now. He treated her well, yes, but she'd known from her first job at age thirteen, one never pried too much into the employer's business. That's not what was done nor tolerated.

She leaned over to fasten up her boots. A few more months. She could do this. Her letter to the Garden Belles had been answered promptly, with assurance that they would forward any suitable letters from a potential husband to her so that she could ensure her future happiness. So far, there had been none. No letters, and no offers of future happiness.

Preston had been all she had dreamed of, and being here reminded her of that. She might temporarily have a place to live and people to dote on, but in a few months, she'd be alone, and the very thought of it made her chest and throat tighten in a distressing way.

He would have been her happiness. Could still be, if only he'd just ask her to marry him!

It was a little bit painful, this current existence, Poppy would tell a friend, if she had one to confide in. She could so easily fall in love with Preston—she already had—but he saw her as nothing more than the governess. It was a kind of ache within her she'd never known before.

And it was torturous.

There was a frantic knock at her door, and Poppy startled from her thoughts, and then laughed, knowing exactly who would stand on the other side and what they wanted. "I'm coming," she said, a smile on her face as she crossed the room and opened the door. She glanced down and raised an eyebrow. "Have you both washed your hands and faces?"

Two beaming little girls spun around, and Poppy nodded approvingly at the twins. Both were neat and tidy, and hadn't complained at all for weeks about being so. Gone were the days of muddy dresses and dangling hair ribbons.

"Well then. You look quite presentable. Shall we go find your uncle and prepare for a day of fun?"

"Yes! Let's go," Anna said, dashing down the stairs, Aria right behind her.

Poppy followed them after she'd grabbed her handbag. When she got to the bottom of the stairs, Preston was there, waiting for her.

"I'll be the luckiest man there, with you lovely ladies," he said.

"That includes Poppy, doesn't it?" Anna asked, looking up at her uncle eagerly.

Poppy's cheeks flamed. "Anna," she started.

But Preston's eyes met hers, causing the heat within her face to grow. She was surprised she didn't combust on the spot. The way he was looking at her made the words on her lips vanish.

"Yes," he said, his voice lower than usual, as something in his eyes flickered. "That includes Poppy."

Time seemed to pause, and there was a heavy feeling that hung in the air as he stared at her, his eyes searching her face, before the twins each grabbed one of his arms and tugged him toward the door.

The spell broken, Poppy inhaled sharply, and followed them outside on her suddenly wobbly legs, closing the door behind her.

What had just happened? She didn't know. Only that she wanted it again. And again, because it was the most incredible feeling she'd ever had that passed through her.

Preston and the girls were waiting for her, and Poppy hurried over, joining them on the walk to the festivities. She enjoyed strolling along with them, passing other families and pretending—just for a moment—that she was with hers. A twinge of guilt ran through her at that. After all, this wasn't her family, and Preston didn't want her there in that capacity. She had no business imagining such a thing.

Aria's small hand snaked into hers, and Poppy looked down, smiling at her. "Are you excited?" she asked.

"I can't wait," Aria said, tugging on her. "Let's hurry!"

"There's plenty of time," Preston said, but Anna had grabbed his hand and pulled on him, and soon they were all nearly jogging to the excitement ahead.

The small town was bustling with lively music playing in the distance and people everywhere. As they drew closer, the scent of popcorn filled Poppy's nose. The twins noticed it too.

"May we get some?" Anna pleaded.

"Of course," Preston said, leading them to the seller, where he bought four paper bags of the fluffy treat.

"Thank you," Poppy said as he handed her one. Their fingers brushed, and she wondered if he'd done that deliberately. But he couldn't have. Not when he'd made it clear he didn't wish to marry.

Still...a small part of her hoped he was changing his mind. After all, hadn't he given her a look that nearly seared her? This life...she could easily see herself living it, so happily. She wanted it so badly.

And she didn't want it with anyone else.

"Over here!" Aria ordered, tugging on her uncle's hand.

They wandered through the fair, watching jugglers with balls and apples and all manner of things flying through the air, and funny clowns with dogs that performed tricks. They clapped and cheered and laughed until they were out of breath at the antics. A small band roamed around, and the twins stopped to dance for a moment, spinning each other about until they were both dizzy.

There were several games set up, and that's where they wandered next. Poppy watched as the girls tried very hard to toss coins into cups to win a prize. She cheered for their attempts, and wrapped her arms around them at their sad faces when all of their tries failed.

Preston took his turn and, thankfully, managed to pitch two of the dimes into containers, winning each of the twins a small prize. Anna chose a lace hanky and Aria a small comb for her dolls. Each seemed pleased with their prize, and hugged him tightly.

"Win your wife a prize?" the man running the game asked.

Poppy flushed, and pretended she hadn't heard the man. Luckily, the twins chose that exact moment to pull Preston toward another booth, one selling jars of candies, and he was also spared having to answer.

Wife. The word was pleasing to her ear, and she wished that she truly was. Was that how people saw them? As a little family? How nice that would be, knowing that at the end of the day, and at the end of her six months there, Preston, and Aria, and Anna would be hers, still, and she would be theirs.

They continued wandering along the fair, enjoying the offerings. They drank freshly made lemonade and ate spiced cookies and chicken legs. When the sun started to dip low, and they walked back toward the house with the twins skipping in front of them, Poppy felt she could hardly breathe as Preston walked right next to her, just inches away.

The silence, and the desire to touch him, was almost unbearable. It had been a nearly perfect day, and she longed for it to never end. More than once, she had seen him looking at her from the corner of her eye. But what had it meant? She wished she knew. Better than that, Poppy wished he'd tell her. And wished it was that he had changed his mind, and wanted her.

"Thank you for inviting me," Poppy finally said, when she couldn't bear the heavy silence another moment. She gave a small laugh as she shook her head. "I had a wonderful time, and I've never been spoiled so thoroughly. You were so wonderfully generous."

Preston didn't answer at first. He was still looking ahead of them, then said, his voice so low she almost didn't hear it, "I wanted to win you a prize as well. But I was worried about how that would look."

In her surprise, Poppy's steps faltered, and she caught up as he stopped. "That's...that's not necessary. I understand, and you don't need to worry about it."

"Poppy," he told her, his voice still low, "I'm sorry."

"What for?" she asked, searching his face for any sort of clue as to why he was apologizing. She kept her own voice quiet, in case he was about to say something he didn't want the twins to overhear.

"For this situation," he told her, sighing softly. "If I may be truthful, you are an incredible woman. I see that. I see how we could be suited. How we might even... But I can't. I'm sorry. Nothing about this is fair, not for anyone. It pains me to think of how the twins will react when you go, and it pains me to feel selfish wanting you to stay for them. For me. When I can't offer you what you want or what you deserve. I wish I could."

Poppy reached out toward his arm, then pulled her fingers back quickly before she touched him. "Can I ask why? You don't—you don't have to tell me. I've no right to know. But..." She couldn't finish. The catch in her throat wouldn't let her.

His sad eyes met hers. "Because I have to protect you," he said quietly. "All of you."

A chill ran up Poppy's arms. That wasn't what she'd expected to hear at all. What she thought he might say, she wasn't sure. That he wasn't ready? That there was someone else? But that...those words that came out of his mouth were just as shocking as his confession had been. The house came into sight then, and as they walked inside, she watched as he vanished, hurrying into his study.

What had he meant, protect them? Did she even want to know? She rubbed her arms, trying to make the goosebumps disappear, but they stayed on her for a long time, just as she stood outside the study, wishing the man she was quickly falling in love with would let her into his heart.

Chapter 13

Preston sat in his desk chair, hunched over, head in hands. He couldn't believe what had just happened, and now he didn't know what to do.

He'd done it. He'd said something to Poppy. It had escaped, even though he'd been doing everything he could the last few weeks to suppress the emotions bubbling up within him. They'd grown so much, though, it was almost like a volcano. Starting first as smoke, then small tendrils of lava slowly burning blazing trails. He had to stop before he erupted and couldn't contain the aftermath.

These feelings were intense. Frightening. Overwhelming. Poppy was all he could think about. What was happening?

Attraction. Affection. Love?

It didn't matter what he called those thoughts and feelings and desires; the fact was his heart, his soul, his everything was full of them. And it was the worst idea in the world. He knew it. But his heart wasn't listening to his mind. He'd never had this problem before. What was so different about Poppy?

He was falling for her. Had fallen for her? Preston wasn't sure. It scared him how much time he wanted to spend with her. How he made excuses to talk to her. Caught himself glancing her way. Trying to please her. Make her happy. He wanted to do that more than anything. He wanted to see that beautiful smile of hers, hear her delighted laugh, watch her eyes shine and know he'd had a small part in making that happen.

But he couldn't.

There was nothing to be done. She had to leave. Leave the town, leave the twins, leave him. If she didn't, he'd end up doing something stupid. Something with potentially dangerous consequences.

Like tell her how much he loved her.

Like kiss her. And ask her to be his wife, be his everything.

He sighed, and glanced at a small pile of letters he'd received with information on several governess candidates from the agency. It was imperative he find a replacement for Poppy, but the ones who had applied wouldn't be suitable for his nieces. He could feel it in each introduction letter sent. The letters spoke of endless rules for the girls; not even a drop of playfulness came through on the page. All the letters were full of sternness, not affection. Of molding them into young ladies, and giving strict lessons, not letting them explore and grow and learn about who they were and what interested them.

All things Poppy encouraged. Her ways worked, as well. He'd never seen the girls so happy, so well behaved. The world was their classroom, and she made learning even the most mundane of things interesting. Why couldn't he find someone just like her as a governess?

But Preston knew the answer to that. There was no one else like Poppy. No one at all. That's why he didn't want to say goodbye and have her leave him. He would miss her too much.

A knock at his study had him hastily sitting up. He smoothed his hair from where his fingers had near been pulling at it. "Yes?" he asked, grabbing his pen and a sheet of paper to look busy. "Come in."

"I'm sorry to disturb you, Mr. Parker," Mrs. Fraser said as she walked toward him. "You've a message. I was told it was urgent."

Preston took the note from her and nodded. He wouldn't look at it until he was alone. "Thank you."

"Did you have an enjoyable time at the fair?" the housekeeper asked. "The girls certainly seemed happy when they came home tonight."

"We did," he answered, unable to stop the smile that came as he thought about all of the moments they had experienced that evening and how much they had all laughed. He wasn't sure the last time he'd allowed himself to relax and spend time doing whatever came to mind. "Those will be good memories, for years to come."

"I'm so glad," Mrs. Fraser said. "If you ask me, you four needed that." She turned and left the room without a backward glance.

Preston sat there, letting those words sink in. Needed it. Yes, he supposed they did. One needed enjoyable times. And that...that had been one of those rare moments where, for a short time, he'd forgotten all his worries. Had felt as though he and the girls and Poppy were a family. It had felt perfect. Right. He'd been so content.

Which was why he had to send her away. If he did, it was one less person to keep safe.

He glanced at the letter in his hand, and opened it, then read it slowly. Sighing, he let it drop from his hand and leaned back in his chair.

Just as he thought. He'd been expecting this. It was good, though. In a way. Preston rapped his knuckles on the table and penned a reply. Folding it, he rose and went in search of Mrs. Fraser.

He found her in the kitchen, having a cup of tea. "Mrs. Fraser, will you see this gets sent for me?" he asked, holding out the note.

"Are you leaving soon?" she asked him, taking the message.

"Tomorrow morning, first thing. I'll be gone for a few days. As long as that gets sent in the morning, it will reach them in time."

She nodded. "I understand. Business as usual for you. At least you got to enjoy yourself tonight."

"Yes," he answered, a smile coming to him as he saw Poppy's smile, so bright as they'd watched the clowns pantomiming, in his mind. "I'm glad for that. Goodnight, and thank you. I'm going to check on the girls and let them know."

"I'll see you in the morning, I suspect. However, if you leave before I do, safe travels," Mrs. Fraser told him.

Preston thanked her and left the kitchen.

As he walked up the stairs to the nursery, where he was sure the three were, one thought only filled his mind. He disliked this. That worried feeling that had started to creep over him. It was hard enough, doing all he could to stay anonymous, to pretend he was someone else so that he could keep the twins a secret. Family could be used against a person. But what choice did he have? He was all they had. He'd done all he could to keep them safe. But it might not have been enough. And now, he had Poppy to worry about too.

He stopped on the stairs and bowed his head. He prayed he was doing the right thing. And that he'd return to them.

Chapter 14

"Girls, I'll be back in a moment," Poppy said, standing from the chair she'd been in, and closing the book she'd been trying, unsuccessfully, to read, ever since Preston had walked in and told them he'd be leaving in the morning.

His eyes had been so worried, that even though almost an hour had passed since he'd told her the news, she couldn't stop thinking about them.

The girls had been sad, but promised to behave and tell him all the things they had done when he returned. It was quite different from the first few times he'd left, when the girls had sobbed and carried on, and begged him to stay.

Was that the reason for the look in his eyes? Poppy didn't think so. He'd had the concern when he first came, and there was a short flicker of relief when the girls had said that. But then something else had come over his face as he hugged them, holding them a little longer than he usually did.

Something was wrong.

The moment she thought that, Poppy knew her instinct was right. But what could it be? Had it to do with what he'd said earlier? About needing to protect them?

A shiver washed over her as she went to the nursery door, trying not to move so swiftly she'd alarm the twins, but still trying to move quickly for her peace of mind.

The twins hardly looked up from the paper they were practicing watercolors on. Poppy paused to admire their work as she crossed the room. Anna was painting the fair they had been to, while Aria was creating a field with flowers. Both girls were focused intently on their artwork. They'd decided to create the paintings the moment their uncle had left the room, hoping to surprise him with them as a parting gift in the morning.

Preston. Poppy's brow furrowed as she moved toward the stairs. The pinched expression on his face had jarred her. And then the way he hugged his nieces tightly—almost too tightly. It was as though he was scared to let them go.

Poppy hurried down the stairs, her hand holding tight to the rail so she didn't trip on her skirt. She just couldn't shake that feeling of concern. She wanted to see him once more. Reassure herself it was nothing. Perhaps the look in his eyes was gone. She could make an excuse to interrupt him. Perhaps thank him again for the evening. Or ask if he wanted the girls to study anything in particular while he was gone.

But she'd also come to a decision, and before he rushed out in the morning, departing for whatever place he was heading toward, she wanted to tell him.

It, oddly, hadn't been a difficult decision at all. Which confused Poppy. Each time she replayed the memories of the day and the conversations she'd had in the last month with Preston, she knew. Her decision might be based on emotion, the very opposite of how she usually was, but her heart agreed with it.

As she'd sat there trying to read, the singular thought kept dancing through her mind. She couldn't leave. She couldn't leave him, couldn't leave the twins. They belonged together. Even if it came at a cost to her. The sacrifice of staying would be great, but Poppy was willing to bear it.

What did that mean for her? Oh, she knew what it meant. A lifetime of loving someone, silently. Maybe that's what he meant by protecting her. He already had a woman he loved. It could even be a forbidden love. Maybe he'd heard from her through the post, and that's why he looked so sad when they came back. They knew they could never be, so he'd rather—just like she would—have nothing than to lose that hope of a future one day. Even if deep inside she knew that nothing would change.

Loving someone who didn't see you the same way. And without them knowing. Could she do that? Be there, always longing for him, for Preston, not for the man who she'd come out to marry, a fictional character who traveled and would give her a life of ease.

If it meant having him in some small way, then yes. She could. Poppy wanted Preston. The loving uncle who cared so deeply for his nieces, and for her, that he kept secrets to spare them pain. The man who worked and worried tirelessly about everyone and everything to ensure their lives were easy.

She wished she knew what those worries were that caused the creases on his brow and the lines around his eyes at such a young age. Perhaps she could ease some of them. Poppy wasn't sure if she'd be able to, but she wanted to try. She longed to help in some way. Even if that meant staying until the twins no longer needed her, and suffering a permanent heartache, as she watched Preston live his life without her.

Eventually, she could move on. Find somewhere else to go. Someone to be with. Perhaps she'd even have a second chance at love. A few years of a delay wouldn't matter. Not really.

A glimpse, she tried to tell herself, a glimpse of him each day would be enough. The brush of their shoulders or fingers as they stood nearby. The smile she put on his face when she said something funny. A look of concern, when he inquired if she was well. She longed for all of those things, even if they'd not be in a more intimate nature, but merely one of friendship.

If she was wrong, and it wasn't enough, and it didn't ease that emptiness inside of her, then Poppy would just manage it anyway. Somehow. She always had. This would be no different.

To be without him would be unbearable, but Poppy well knew that life was often filled with those moments. The times when one either needed to curl up and wither away, or continue on, forging a new path, even if it wasn't quite what one had dreamed of.

She could still travel. Meet people. Perhaps even find someone who erased all thoughts of Preston from her mind if she didn't just apply to another matchmaking agency. It was unlikely, especially as she became advanced in years, but it wasn't unheard of.

Poppy stood at the bottom of the stairs, and glanced around for him. Perhaps he was in his study. She hoped he was. While she was feeling brave enough, and while her longing and desire for him could still be tamped down to spare her all the heartache possible, she wanted to speak with him.

Poppy drew closer and saw the door ajar. She walked toward it, intending to knock, when she heard a voice she didn't recognize coming through the crack.

"Make sure you're discreet."

"I always am," Preston answered. "Are you sure this time? The information I got last month wasn't accurate. You know the risk if there's a mistake and what could happen."

"Oh yeah. We've been watching real close. Had the place under surveillance for two weeks now. Easy in, easy out," the second voice said. "Just don't you get caught."

Caught? Caught at what? Poppy creeped closer to the door, standing at an angle to better see what was happening. This sounded serious. Was this part of why he was worried? But where was he about to go? What was he about to do?

"I don't intend to," Preston said. "There's too much at stake."

"Don't forget this," the second man said. "It's clean. Can't be traced."

Poppy gasped, and her hands flew over her mouth. From the crack in the door, she witnessed the man handing a revolver to Preston. He opened the chamber, nodded, and tucked it into his inner jacket pocket.

A gun. Preston was just given a gun? But why? Shivers came over her, and she longed to turn away, pretend she'd not heard anything, but that wouldn't be right. She was determined to learn all she could. Her life might depend on it, especially if she had to run for the law.

"Take care of the problem," the man growled. "You know what's at stake. The boss isn't going to be happy if this keeps dragging on."

"You think I'm not trying? I've been working this for almost a year. I want it as badly as anyone." Preston stepped toward the door.

Poppy rapidly backed up. What had she just seen and heard? Her heart thudded wildly. She'd been wrong all along, hadn't she? Preston hadn't been trying to protect his nieces or her from an unrequited love or heartbreak. That also wasn't why he didn't want to marry her.

It was because he was a criminal!

Chapter 15

Preston dug through his desk, looking for some of his travel cash. As he straightened and closed the door, he checked for his train ticket, and chuckled to himself. It had been a while since he'd put on his shoes and found shaving foam in them or reached into a pocket and found a worm or a snake or a frog.

He wouldn't say he missed those days, exactly, and there were many times it had been annoying or frustrating, especially when he'd been in a hurry or had a guest over and the pranks embarrassed him or the guest. But some of the twins' tricks had been humorous, and just the sort of thing he'd done himself as a boy. Not that he'd mention that to them. It wouldn't do to encourage the behavior.

While the twins were still always sad to see him leave, he could tell they were quite happy having Poppy there, and less worried about being without him. It helped with his stress, as he knew that they'd be well taken care of, and that Poppy would—did—love them as her own.

Poppy. He'd meant to ask her last night if she'd consider staying longer than the six months, if that's what it took to find a governess. However, when he went to look for her after Stevens had left, her bedroom door was shut. He didn't want to bother her if she was sleeping, so he had walked away.

Concern grew each day over the situation of a replacement for her. Not that anyone could replace Poppy. She was beautiful, cheerful, clever, witty, compassionate, attentive... He could go on and on, but it wouldn't be wise.

But, he simply had to have a governess. More importantly, he needed to have a good one. One who would treat the girls well. Though he'd received eleven letters of recommendation for governesses, not a single one felt right. And with what he had to do now... just in case something were to happen to him, he wanted the assurance the girls would be looked after. That's why, even if she didn't need to stay beyond the six months she'd agreed to, he was hoping that she might.

Just the idea of having her there would relieve some of the worry in his mind, and help him concentrate better while he was gone.

He sighed as he glanced around his study. Hopefully, he'd be back in a few days. The entire situation made him feel nervous. That feeling that something just wasn't right filled him, and he wished he didn't have to go, and could stay to protect the girls, even if it was just from the shadows on their nursery wall.

He left the room and headed toward the front door, his travel bag in hand. Mrs. Fraser stopped him as his hand twisted the knob.

"Mr. Parker," she said. "Thank goodness I've caught you. The train's stopped. You won't be able to leave just yet."

"Stopped? As in, it's not running?"

"Yes. Some rail damage down the line, I was told. Men are trying to repair it now, but it will be hours at a minimum. Little Danny, the stationmaster's son, promises to come get you when they know when it will be boarding. He knows that you were leaving on it and promises it won't go without you."

"I see. I guess that gives me a little more time here," Preston said, knitting his brow. He wondered what had caused the damage, and of what type it was. It could be something simple. Occasionally, a piece or two of the track did come up and needed to be repaired, but that never took too long. Nothing that would take hours.

Was this sabotage? Not everyone liked the idea of a train coming through. Several had suspicions about it, didn't care for the noise of the men building, the shaking and the whistle of the train, the land it cut through. There were always those against what they didn't like, but not all were content with only being vocal about it. Some took to violence or destruction of property that wasn't theirs.

While most folks favored the railroad, and the swift travel it afforded, a good number did not, and some did try to damage the tracks. Rival companies had also been known to indulge in sabotage, which was why—

"Oh! Forgive me," Poppy said, as she nearly walked into him. "I was distracted."

"Quite all right," Preston assured her, glad to see her. "I was as well. Actually, I was hoping to talk with you before I left. Things worked out so that I could, since my train has been delayed."

"Talk with me?" She took on a suddenly nervous expression, which confused him. Very little seemed to shake her. Why had this?

Poppy smoothed her hands down her dress, then plucked at the cuff on one sleeve. "About what?"

"Come into my study," he said, leading the way. "I want to show you something and get your opinion."

Poppy followed him down the hallway, where he went into his study and to his desk. Opening the second drawer of his desk, he pulled the stack of letters out from the Gardner Nanny Agency and dropped them on the desktop. "Here. What do you think?" he asked. "Open them."

She did, slowly at first, as if unsure what she'd find, then she quickly began to skim the letters, one after the other, wearing a tiny frown that he found adorable on her lips.

"This is the best they could find?" she asked, sounding irritated as she waved a letter. "I wouldn't want to leave an animal with some of these women. Let alone two young girls." She shook her head. "Not a single one addressed the fact that the girls are orphans and need a gentle touch, as they've been through so much."

"I agree," he sighed. "I've sent another letter telling them that not one of these women is suitable, and explaining, again, what it is the girls must have. The problem is, though I've been specific about what I want and what the girls need, this is the sort of thing they keep sending me. Are all governesses like this?" He was sure he sounded frustrated, and hoped Poppy wouldn't think it was directed toward her.

"A good deal are," Poppy said. "That is what some employers want. Strict. Someone who will make the children behave at all times. I guess...in that regard, I'm not very governess-like."

"You are far better for them than the whole lot of these women combined," Preston said hotly, gesturing at the discarded letters.

He was rewarded with a small smile as she put the last letter she was holding back in its envelope. "What will you do? The girls must have someone who will care for them."

"Keep looking. But I wanted you to know that I was," Preston told her. "I also wondered..." He stopped. He'd almost said the one thing that he didn't want to say. That he was in love with her and didn't want her to leave. That he wanted her to stay with him for the rest of her life and his. To be together and share laughter and smiles and hold hands and...and anything else she wanted. So long as she would stay.

But he couldn't say that. Not a single word of it.

Poppy was still waiting, and Preston took a breath. No, he must ask the other thing he also hesitated to ask, but needed to, for peace of mind before he left. "I wondered, if I can't find someone, will you consider staying longer?"

"Longer." Her voice was flat.

Preston hurried to add, "I know what we agreed. I do. Six months only. I'm sorry. You do see I'm trying. I just can't do that to the girls. Not after they've had someone like you. And, I can't leave Mrs. Fraser with them. She has the house to run. She's also getting older, though she won't admit it. It's too much on her to care for the twins and the house.

"My travel schedule can be unpredictable, and when I'm home, as you know, I do a great deal of work in my study. I need someone to watch the girls. Someone who I know will love them the way I do, and care for them, and treat them how they should be treated. Fairly."

She still didn't answer. Preston wasn't sure what to say. How could he persuade her? He wasn't sure more money was what she wanted. But he'd offer it, if he needed to. In fact, he'd offer most anything to get Poppy to stay there with hi—with the girls.

But was that true? Would he? Preston knew the thing she wanted most. To be married. But he couldn't offer that. Especially when he wasn't sure he'd be able to return home to her and the girls after today.

Poppy slowly walked to the window that overlooked the garden. The same one that, on her first day, he'd stared out of, watching her. Starting to fall in love with her before he'd even realized it.

What would she say? Preston decided to beg, if that's what it took. Plead. Get on his knees. He'd do anything. Anything except tell her the truth, that was. So, when he opened his mouth and the words fell out, he didn't know what to do. How would she take them? In an innocent way? Or the way his heart meant them?

"Poppy, please don't go. Don't leave me. I need you."

Chapter 16

Poppy didn't dare turn around. She wasn't sure what Preston would see on her face. In all of her years, she wasn't sure she'd ever felt so confused, or horrified, or frightened, or...well, there was a lot. She couldn't quite decide which emotion was winning for dominance.

Night after night for the last few months, she'd analyzed each word, each moment, each thought that had come from him. This one was the same. But, perhaps even the most difficult to decipher of all.

"I need you."

What did he mean? Was he saying that, as in he needed her as the governess for the twins? Or because *he* needed *her*? Poppy was burning to know. Had those words come before she'd witnessed him in the study, heard the chilling words, "Take care of the problem," and seen him with a weapon capable of hurting someone within an instant, she might be reacting differently. As it was, right now she was wondering how freely she should speak.

Poppy studied him. The lines of worry etched near his eyes and on his forehead. The tension in his shoulders and arms. The swirling emotions that flashed on his face. What did it mean?

Was her life in danger? Were the twins? She could leave. Take them to safety. Hide them. Get help from a lawman, protect Anna and Aria. That might be the best thing to do. The right thing to do.

But...though her head was telling her that might be one option for her, there was another voice telling her that she might be overreacting. If Preston were a criminal, wouldn't Mrs. Fraser have noticed? Have had concerns? She was a good woman; surely she wouldn't have let those girls be around someone like that.

But then... what if she hadn't realized it? Poppy's eyes narrowed as she studied him, deep in thought. After all, Poppy had been here for several months, and never once had she suspected him of being anything more than how he presented himself. A good, honest, and hardworking businessman, and a loving uncle who doted on the children he was guardian over.

Perhaps his charade was so good that no one had noticed. Not even her. It was simply by chance she'd learned what she had.

What should she do?

Her pulse sped up, and Poppy pulled her lower lip between her teeth. He was waiting for an answer. She had to give him one. She couldn't pretend she hadn't heard him. Her gaze went outside the window again, as if there might be an answer there for her among the grass and trees and flowers.

There wasn't. But she sensed him stepping closer to her. Heard his shoes on the wooden floor.

Poppy finally turned, half scared about what she might see. Preston with a weapon in his hand? An angry look in his eyes? Another man there, waiting to drag her away if she refused? What if he threatened the safety of the girls?

No, he wouldn't do that. A person couldn't pretend the affection that he'd shown his nieces. That made her feel slightly better, though her pulse was still racing.

Slowly, she dragged her eyes from the small carpet by his desk to his shoes, and reluctantly to his face. There, she saw something new carved into his features. Desperation, almost. The familiar lines and creases, perhaps a little deeper than before. His eyes were searching hers, looking for her answer. Trying to figure out what to say. The gesture was so familiar, so Preston, harboring that uncertainty he often had when talking to her, that she relaxed further.

"Poppy," he began, "I promise you, I'll figure something out. I know you don't want to stay. It's just I'm worried about the twins. I can't explain more or what I do for a living. But, sometimes, it could put me in danger. Put them in danger, if they don't have a caregiver I trust and something were to happen to me. Right now, that person, the only person I trust to take care of them, is you."

"So, my staying is only for the twins?" Poppy asked, surprised at her boldness, and slightly embarrassed that her voice had the smallest of wobbles. Had he noticed it? Surely he had, but right now she didn't care.

Preston's face filled with surprise. Before he could answer, Poppy pressed forward, pushing that shame down deep inside. She had a question, and she wanted an answer to it. Nothing would stop her. Even if it was to be the end of her, she wanted to know. Deserved to know.

"You said you need me. Is that only to be the caregiver of Anna and Aria? Or is it because *you* need me? You, Preston, not the girls. I'm asking about you. I know you didn't want to marry. Have you...have you changed your mind? About a wife? About me?"

His shoulders stiffened, and a muscle in his jaw twitched. Poppy wasn't sure what that meant. Preston ran a hand through his hair, nervously. "Poppy," he said, half whispering. "I...I can't. I can't answer."

She stepped closer, that boldness filling her to the point where Poppy almost felt as though she wasn't in control of her actions at all. Or her words. At this moment, she wasn't sure who she was, other than a woman who wanted answers.

"Why not?" she asked, the question spilling out of her. "You can't answer or you won't? The night of the fair, you made it sound as though you might be feeling something for me. Before that, there were other moments too. I think my question deserves an answer before I give you mine."

Poppy was sure her eyes were fierce. Her voice sounded like it to her ears. She was shocked at her actions, but, though she'd fully intended to love Preston the rest of her life without him knowing, his actions in the study with the man she'd heard him talking to had changed things. Made her feel bolder. As though time were much shorter, and there was none to waste.

He swallowed hard. "Yes."

"Yes, what?" Poppy asked. "That I deserve an answer, or that, yes, you need me?"

Preston closed his eyes. When he opened them, Poppy nearly trembled at the burning look on his face, and took a half step back. "Yes, Poppy, I need you. I want you. You, here. Even if it's not as the governess. I want you in any way that I can have you, because without you my life would be empty, there would be a hole in my soul, and I would spend every minute the rest of my life missing you. But, right now, that's all I can offer you. Being here as the governess. Don't you see?"

He turned away from her, agitatedly, and paced the room, a few steps one way and then back again. "Why are you asking? Pressing? I told you. I can't. I have to protect you. All of you. The less you know, the better I can do that."

Poppy stopped his restless steps, blocking his path and shocking herself at her nearness to him. Slowly, as though she were afraid that either he or she would bolt from the action, she rested her fingertips lightly on his arm and looked deeply into his eyes. "Because I just want to know if I've fallen in love with a criminal, and if he loves me too."

Chapter 17

Preston's jaw dropped. It felt like the breath had been knocked out of him. His mouth snapped shut as he started to sputter. Finally, after several fits and starts, he managed, "What are you talking about? A criminal? Me?"

Poppy studied him for a long moment, then nodded. "Yes. I went to look for you last night, and as I was walking toward your study, I heard another man in there. The door was slightly ajar, and I saw that he handed you a gun. And told you to take care of the problem."

Realization washed over him, and Preston would have laughed had she not looked so serious. "I see." Then, the other thing she'd said sank in, and Preston whispered, "Wait." He swallowed hard. "You...you love me? It's not that you just want to marry me to be married? You...you also love me?"

Her back straightened, and her long red braid swung over her shoulder. "I do."

Once more, Preston found himself speechless. He reached his hands out toward her, but then dropped them again. "Oh, Poppy," he sighed, and then led her to the small sofa in his study. As they settled down, he said, "I'm not sure where to start."

"With your first crime, of course," Poppy said, in that matter-of-fact way of hers that struck him as so perfectly delightful. "I want to hear the entire sordid tale. Then, I'll decide what I'm going to do."

The expression on her face was so serious, he couldn't help it. Preston laughed. That made her scowl, as she said, "I don't find this humorous."

"Forgive me," Preston said, managing to stop the chuckles with quite a bit of effort. "My first crime... Does stealing cookies as a child count?" The scowl grew, and Preston wondered at how it made her even more beautiful. Her eyes were snapping at him now, and he longed to lean forward and kiss her. He felt so light, right now. So happy.

As Poppy opened her mouth, he held up a hand. "I'm not what you think," he told her.

"That's abundantly obvious," she retorted. "Which is why I'm waiting to hear just what you've gotten yourself mixed up in before I decide if I want to be around it."

"I mean, I'm not a criminal," Preston said. "I'm a railway detective."

Poppy raised a brow, but didn't answer. He sighed. "It's true. I've been trying for the last year, almost a year and a half now, to track down who has been committing crimes at the railway company I work for. That's why I travel, sometimes for weeks on end. I'm following clues and trying to intercept the individual or group responsible. So far," he sighed, and rubbed at his jaw, "I've not been able to catch them."

"I see," she said slowly. "That seems a monumental task for one person."

"I've a team of six beneath me," he told her. "The man you overheard was my second in command. Bert Stevens. He's as frustrated as I am by not being able to catch the man."

"What kind of attacks?" Poppy asked. "Damaging the tracks?"

"That usually tends to be done by those against the railroad expanding too near to their lands," he told her. "We have no reason to believe those instances are connected, as what I am investigating is more costly. Theft of payroll, items and damage in Pullman cars during the short duration they are empty, cargo missing. That sort of thing. I had a close call the last time I came back. Had it not been for Bert, I may not have returned at all. I was attacked, and all we got was the overcoat of the man who did it. We suspect that it's a criminal ring.

"One of my other men ran after the one who attacked me, and he's still in the hospital. The office where employee files are kept was also ransacked, and there's some concern that my information, as well as my men's, was discovered. We all have families, and are desperate to stop the thefts, get these individuals locked up, and protect our loved ones."

She was quiet for a long moment. "No wonder you have been so worried," she said. "Not just in general, but also about someone to care for the girls. Do you suspect..." she hesitated a long moment before finishing, "do you suspect one day you might not return?"

"Yes," he said softly, admitting one of the fears he had, "or else someone discovering that I have the girls, and coming after them. Coming after you."

Preston closed his eyes a moment. It felt good to finally unburden himself. To not carry such a deep fear alone. When he opened them, he whispered, "Poppy, I couldn't bear that. I don't want you hurt. I don't want the girls hurt. By keeping my distance, I can keep you safe."

"But what about what I want?" Poppy asked. "Don't I get a say?"

That took him aback. Of all the things that he thought she'd say, that wasn't one of them. "Of course," he said, blinking several times.

She shook her head. "Oh, Preston, I don't know what to do. Do you know, last night I went looking for you to tell you that I'd stay for the girls. I was going to stay as long as you needed me because I'm in love with you. I wasn't going to tell you that part, not then and not now, but of course, it slipped out.

"I figured if...if I had you, even from afar, that might be enough. That I could be happy. But I realize it's not and it could never be. I understand you have a dangerous job. But I want to be here for you if you need me. To help make your burdens lighter. Be the person you talk to when you need it. Then, there's also the matter now, of if something were to happen to you. A wife could legally care for the twins still, as a guardian. A governess could be dismissed by whoever assumed control over them—and their trust fund."

Preston didn't quite know what to say. He hadn't thought about that, how even if he'd asked Poppy to stay, she'd have no control over her future. She was very practical minded, and he should have expected nothing less.

Again, he noticed how Poppy wasn't asking for anything. She was being selfless, and wonderful, and all of the things he just wasn't used to. But they were all of the things that he had wanted. She spoke the truth as well. Especially about the twins' trust fund. Who would their next of kin be to care for them? It was likely it wouldn't be someone who would love them the way he did, especially as he didn't know who they were.

Before he could say more, she continued, "Even if you don't marry me, I want you to know that I love you. I want to be your friend and your companion, and make you smile. I want to see Anna and Aria grow up, because I love all of you. I want to be with you, for each moment that you'll have me, no matter in what way. I love you each so dearly and don't want to ever say goodbye."

There was a catch in her final words, and Preston couldn't hold himself back. He pulled Poppy close to him, and wrapped his arms tightly around her. "I've fallen in love too. With you, Poppy."

Chapter 18

Poppy had never been embraced the way Preston was holding her. She felt as though she were the most important, the most treasured thing imaginable. If she could, she'd stay there forever. Her body felt warm and fuzzy, her heart near bursting with joy. She could hardly believe what he'd just said.

He had fallen in love with her. Her. But...what did that mean? For her, for Preston, for the future? Especially with all he'd just told her about his job and the danger it entailed. Poppy's brows knit together in concern. She'd need to ask him. Just because he loved her didn't mean he'd do anything about it.

She drew back slightly, just enough to better see him. His eyes were warm, and his expression one she'd never seen before. His hand rose to her cheek, and she sighed softly, dropping her face into his palm. "Preston—"

"Uncle Preston! Where are you?"

Anna's scream of absolute terror filled the room. As one, Poppy and Preston ran to the study door, just as Anna and Aria burst in, expressions of fear on their faces.

"What happened?" Preston demanded, leaning down to wrap his arms around the girls. They clung to him, shaking, and their words jumbled. Poppy couldn't understand anything they were saying.

"Slow down," Preston said, his voice ringing with an authority Poppy had never heard him use on the twins.

"There's a man," Aria gasped out, pointing toward the window.

"What kind of a man?" Poppy asked. Fear filled her as she moved to the window, hoping to spot whoever it was who had spooked the girls. Had the person Preston was looking for arrived there?

Her eyes met his overtop the twins' heads, and before he looked back at the girls, Poppy found herself wondering how he'd managed to carry such a burden himself for so long. She'd only known for a few moments, and she was terrified for their safety.

And determined no one would hurt these children. With her final breath, she'd protect them. This must be what Preston felt. Why he didn't want to do anything that could risk them.

"A strange man. We'd never seen him before. We were setting up for a tea party," Anna started.

"I put down the teacups," Aria said, miming the action with her small hands. "When I turned around to go to the kitchen for cookies, a man was in the garden."

"*In* the garden," Anna shrieked. "He came from inside the shed."

Poppy watched as Preston's hand went into his jacket's inner pocket. She wondered if he was looking for the revolver he'd been given by Bert. She was glad now that he had it.

"What did he look like?" Preston asked, moving toward the study door.

"He had a dirty hat and a brown jacket," Anna said.

"And he was asking questions. Like where you were," Aria said, her voice still high-pitched from fright. "He kept asking where you were."

"I want you to go upstairs," Preston said, his voice tight. "The three of you. Hide. Don't come out until I say."

Preston met Poppy's eyes once more. Though her heart was pounding, she nodded firmly. No one would hurt the girls. Not while she was breathing.

"Girls, come with me," she said, quickly grabbing their hands. "Upstairs. While your uncle investigates, we will do the prudent thing as he has asked. Stay out of the way and hide."

The twins hurried along, with no further prompting needed. Poppy went behind them, shielding them from anyone who might come in from the front, and hoping they made it to the nursery in time. There was no lock on the door to the nursery. As a matter of fact, none of the rooms but Preston's study had a lock, as far as she knew, but there were places she could have the girls hide. Both were excellent hide and seek players, so she was sure they knew of places she didn't.

"I'm scared," Anna whimpered.

"Me too," Aria sobbed.

Poppy hurried them into the nursery, then knelt before the girls. "Listen," she said firmly. "While I'm sure there's nothing to be worried about, we will do what your uncle has asked."

"What if it's the bad man he's been trying to get?" Anna asked, rubbing at her eyes with the back of her hand. "What if he's come for us?"

"You know about that?" Poppy asked in surprise.

"Of course. Papa was a detective too," Aria said. "That might be why he was killed. Mama too. Uncle Preston has always been worried about that."

"Though he wouldn't come out and say it," Anna finished. She shared a look with her sister.

Poppy sucked in a deep breath and sat back on her knees. The girls were far more aware of things than she'd realized. It did break her heart, though, that they had been carrying that concern about their parents being murdered, and perhaps them being next.

"I see. Goodness, the next time I am curious about something, I will come ask you," she said with a small laugh. Poppy thought for a moment. "Well," she said slowly. "I've only just learned all this myself today. What your uncle does, I mean."

"We must help him," Anna cried, her calm demeanor gone.

"We can't lose Uncle!" Aria said, her voice one of panic. "But what do we do?"

"You must listen to what he's asked you to do," Poppy said firmly. "Girls, this is one of those times where there could be a dangerous consequence if you don't listen. You are the most important things in the world to him. He wants you safe. If you don't do as he's asked, it may put him in danger."

Both girls nodded, their eyes fixed on her. "How can we stay safe?" Anna asked.

"What do we do, Poppy?" Aria pleaded.

Poppy's eyes darted around the room. There must be something there for them to defend themselves with, if it came down to that.

A shiver ran through her. This fear she felt must be in some small way what Preston felt every day. A worry that his worst nightmare would come true. That the twins would be put in danger because of him, because of his job.

She was scared for him. What if he found the man and was overpowered? What if there was more than one? He had mentioned a criminal gang. Had he been shot? Dragged away? And what might happen to the girls without a parent? She had been right that a governess couldn't become their guardian.

She understood why he wanted her to stay. Though they'd not figured out yet in what capacity, Poppy knew it didn't matter. Nothing at all mattered but being there for Preston and protecting the girls. He needed her, and so did they. She wouldn't leave them unless they asked her to.

"Girls, what do you see from the windows?" Poppy asked, as determination to take care of this small family filled her.

Each of the twins ran to a window and peered out. Poppy started to search the room. There wasn't much she could use to barricade the door. The girls had books and dolls, blocks, and art supplies. Nothing they could use to protect themselves. Why would they?

She still moved the small table the girls drew at against the closed nursery door. It was better than nothing. If nothing else, it would buy a moment. Maybe there was something else heavy to put on top of it.

"I don't see anything," Anna said.

"There's a man running to the house," Aria screamed. "It's not Uncle Preston! I don't see him anywhere."

That settled it.

"Girls, we may need to defend ourselves," Poppy said firmly, snatching up the fire poker. Chills washed over her, but she ignored them. "You will stay behind me. If I fall or get taken, get outside. Scream. Go for help. Do not stop to help me, do you understand? I will hold him off for as long as I can."

It was the truth, as well. Poppy knew she'd give her everything, with no thought to the consequences for herself, if it meant the twins could escape.

"Poppy," Aria whispered.

"We love you," Anna said.

"I love you too," Poppy said as tears pricked at her eyes. Then she squared her shoulders. "Are you ready, girls? We will not go down without a fight."

Anna ran toward a pile of blocks, while Aria seized the small stool from their child-sized table. Both stood bravely, even with tears and fear evident on their faces.

Somehow, over the loud thudding of her heart that echoed in her ears, Poppy could hear the front door slam. Poppy stood to the side of the door, ready for whoever it was that would surely be bursting in. The fire poker felt cold and heavy in her trembling hands, but she raised it, ready to swing with all she had in her. She would buy the twins time to escape.

Footsteps, loud, heavy, and fast thundered up the stairs. Everything went quiet, and Poppy realized she was holding her breath. She forced herself to breathe out slowly. It would do her no good if she passed out. She had to breathe in. Out. In. Ou—

The doorknob jiggled.

Chapter 19

The last glimpse Preston had of his nieces and Poppy was as they were rushing up the stairs, Poppy shielding them from behind. He prayed they'd find a place to hide, and that whoever it was outside wasn't there to harm them. Perhaps it was a workman. Someone lost.

But Aria had said the man was asking questions about him. Had been inside the shed. That meant the person had to have been poking around, had known about him, and the girls by default. He had always been so careful, though. Where had he made a mistake? Was his information stolen when the railway office was broken into?

He glanced about for Mrs. Fraser, to warn her that the worst might have happened, when he remembered it was Tuesday, the day she did the food shopping. She wasn't home. He remembered how just after she'd told him the train was delayed, she'd left. That was both a relief and a worry. What if she walked into something? But that also meant he had no one to send for help.

He wondered now, if the delay in his departure was due to the man lurking about. Had he or his men sabotaged the train tracks? And to what purpose? To come after him? The girls?

Thoughts of his brother and his sister-in-law filled his mind. Their deaths had been ruled an accident, but he'd always wondered. Worried. He'd likely never get to know just what happened, but he knew he'd never, not as long as he had a breath left in his body, let their daughters come to harm.

"I will protect them," he whispered, as Poppy, Aria, and Anna flashed through his mind.

Carefully, he peered through the windows at the front of the house. He didn't see anyone. He moved from room to room, glancing this way and that, while also making sure the doors and windows were locked. Where was the man? Was he alone? He turned, about to move to a new window, when a flicker appeared in the corner of his eye. There! A movement in the back garden area. A man was coming out of the small shed where the garden tools were kept. His back was to Preston, but he could see, just as Anna said, the man was wearing a brown jacket and a dirty hat.

Preston pulled the revolver from his pocket and slipped through the kitchen door, keeping close to the side of the house for protection. He approached the garden, gun firmly in hand as he peered around the corner of the house. The man was gone. He went through the garden gate and looked through the small window in the shed. No one was inside. Nothing looked disturbed either, not that there was much in there.

Where had the man gone? Preston hurried around the perimeter of the house. No one. He knew the man hadn't gotten inside. The front door was locked, and he hadn't taken his eyes off of the kitchen door as he'd searched for the man for more than a few seconds.

A sudden noise caught his attention, and Preston saw the man with the brown jacket on the front porch. He'd tripped, and was righting himself. Preston could hardly believe his luck.

"Stop there," Preston growled, and he drew closer. "Hands up, nice and slow."

The man did just that, but then suddenly spun around just as Preston came within reach, sending a punch aimed directly at him. However, Preston was ready, and met the other man's momentum, deflecting it by spinning away. He'd just moved in close to wrestle the man to the ground when the hat on the other man's head fell and he froze. "Bert?"

"Preston!" the detective said, dropping the elbow he'd raised. "Thank goodness. You took me by surprise."

"Me? I almost knocked you out!" Preston said. "What are you playing at? Why are you still here? I thought we were going to meet."

"I was there," Bert answered quickly, holding his hands up. "We got the man last night. I hurried here as fast as I could. Took the overnight train and intended to ride with you this morning as we did the final paperwork to call it a day. I was so tired though, and it was about four this morning when I got here. I didn't want to disturb you, so I let myself in your shed. Must have dozed off deeper than I realized, for when I woke up, those nieces of yours were about to play with their dollies."

"You scared them quite a bit," Preston said, putting the revolver back into his jacket. "Me as well."

"I didn't mean to," Bert said apologetically. "I'll tell them so. It was you I wanted, and so I tried to pretend I was a workman. Just asking where you were, you know? I couldn't think of any other reason for coming out of your garden shed. I don't think they believed me, though."

"They didn't, but it got me here," Preston chuckled, feeling much better now that he realized no one had been at risk. "I'd best let them know all is well."

"Poor mites. I really am sorry," Bert said, pushing his hat up to rub at his forehead.

"What matters is that it was a false alarm," Preston said. "So, how'd you catch the man?"

"We waited for him. Set the bait, just as you'd suggested. Silver coins, a whole lot of them, not bars. Greedy man, stood there filling his pockets and didn't even notice us. It was the quickest and easiest thing we'd ever done."

"He was alone?" Preston asked. "What of his sister? The cleaning woman who tipped him off?"

"She wasn't there, but he had two friends as lookouts," Bert explained. "The police caught them. Wanted for all sorts of crimes, they were. I suspect it will be a quick trial and a favorable outcome for the railroad. His sister should have known better. They sang like birds to tell us where she lived, and she was arrested at her home."

"Sometimes we do things for family we know we shouldn't. I just hope the stolen property is recovered," Preston said. "The sum of what they stole was not insignificant. Nor was the damage done to the Pullman cars from the theft."

"When this hits the papers, it will make others think twice before attempting such a thing themselves," Bert added. "Crime doesn't pay, not for long."

"That's something we both agree on," Preston said. "Want to come in for a bite and a bit of a rest?"

"No. Thank you, though. Now that that's all taken care of, I want to head back home, let the missus know I'm well so she stops worrying. You know how it is." Bert gave a wave as he walked away. "Next time."

Preston waved his own hand in farewell and turned to the door. He was glad he'd be able to tell the girls and Poppy all was well. He hoped they weren't too frightened.

He hurried into the house and called for them. "Poppy? Anna? Aria?" When there was no answer, he grew worried. Had Bert been wrong and someone had gotten past them?

He ran up the stairs, fear growing inside of him with every step he climbed.

Chapter 20

There was hardly time to blink and steel herself before the door slowly opened. When it opened further, Poppy let out a cry, and swung the poker. She struck air, but pulled the iron rod back to her shoulder to ready herself for another attempt.

Meanwhile, wooden blocks began to fly through the air at the intruder, and Anna and Aria were letting out what sounded like battle cries.

"Stop! Stop! It's me!" a familiar voice shouted, as the door tried to close to give the person protection.

Narrowing her eyes, Poppy tried to see who it was calling out to them, but the door wasn't open wide enough to make them out.

Several blocks hit the closed door before Aria asked, "Wait. Was that Uncle Preston?"

"Yes, lamb, it's me," her uncle called through the door, his voice slightly muffled.

"Oh no!" Poppy dropped the poker with a clang, and jerked the door open. She stared in horror at Preston. "I'm sorry. Thank goodness I didn't hit you."

"I agree," he said dryly. "Thank goodness. I wasn't expecting to be attacked by the fireplace poker or the block set." He raised his brows and took in the scene before him. "Aria! Were you about to throw that chair at me?"

Poppy gave a sheepish shrug, while the twins didn't even try to hide their laughter. Before she could say anything, he smiled. "It seems you ladies are capable of defending yourselves quite well."

"I'm awfully glad we didn't hurt you," Anna said. Then, she proudly asked, "How was my aim?"

"Astonishingly good, duck," he answered. "Is it safe for me to come in now?"

The twins ran to their uncle, hugging him tightly. Poppy, however, couldn't feel relief yet. "What's happened?" she asked. "Is it safe? Who was the man?"

"Don't worry, Uncle Preston," Anna said. "You can say it in front of us."

"We know you are a detective and chase bad men," Aria added.

Preston gave a sigh and shook his head. "I see. You two figured it out, did you? I should have known you would, the way you two sneak about."

"It's in our blood, Mrs. Fraser says," Anna said, while Aria nodded solemnly.

Preston explained, "That was Bert. He works for me. All is well. Last night, the ones responsible for the thefts were caught. He had come to tell me, but as it was in the wee hours of the morning, decided to wait until a reasonable time to let me know. He waited in the garden shed so no one would think he was lurking about. However, he dozed off, and when he woke, the girls were there, and he needed to find me, in hopes I'd not already left."

"I see," Poppy said. "Why didn't he simply come to the door and knock?"

"I think he didn't wish to disturb anyone," Preston told her. "However, that certainly didn't go according to his plan, did it?"

"No, it didn't," she agreed. "However, I'm glad everything has worked out. Both in that the criminal has been apprehended and that the person lurking about turned out to be harmless."

"I'm sorry that I kept everything a secret," Preston said, rubbing a hand through his hair. "I hope that you each realize I did it because I didn't want you to be frightened or worried. I also didn't speak about what I did," he fixed the twins with a look, "though you two figured it out, because I wanted to protect you. The more you knew, the greater the likelihood of putting you in danger."

The twins exchanged looks. "We didn't think about that," Anna said.

"Like we didn't think all those other times we did stuff we shouldn't have," Aria said. She looked down at her shoes. "Poppy told us there are consequences when we don't listen or think. Like people could get hurt."

"It's true," Poppy said, wrapping an arm around each of the girls, "but we are fortunate that this time, everything turned out well. Sometimes it doesn't."

"We're sorry, Uncle Preston," Anna said.

"It's all right, duck. I just love you, that's all. It's why I want to protect you. When you care for someone, you want to do all you can to keep them safe."

The twins exchanged glances again, and Aria asked sweetly, a coy look on her face. "Poppy too?"

Poppy was sure her face was red. She also remembered now, they hadn't had a chance to finish their conversation earlier.

"It just so happens that Poppy and I were about to talk about something in regards to that, when all of the excitement happened," Preston said. "How about you two play while Poppy and I finish our conversation?"

Anna promptly crossed her arms.

"Only if that means she's staying, and you aren't replacing her with someone else."

"We don't want those old ladies who keep writing," Aria agreed.

Preston's mouth opened and closed. "How do you know about that?" he asked. "Have you been snooping in my desk?"

"You aren't the only one who is a detective," Poppy laughed. "Mrs. Fraser is quite right. Finding out about things runs in this family. I'd best guard any secrets I have extra carefully!"

She didn't have it in her to scold the girls. Not after the morning they'd had, and especially because she wanted to stay just as much as the girls wanted her.

Preston just shook his head, and left the nursery. A sudden fear filled Poppy, and she saw it on the girls' faces too. Poppy hoped that he was going to tell her what she'd been longing to hear, that he wanted her to marry him, but if he was going to say such a thing, wouldn't he at least have looked differently, without that strained, pinched expression he was wearing?

Perhaps now that he perceived the danger was past, he was going to tell her he didn't need her anymore. Poppy's heart sank to her stomach, and she slowly followed him.

Chapter 21

How was he going to do this? Preston wasn't sure. Earlier, before the twins had burst in with the news of an intruder, the moment had felt right. Perfect, even. He'd felt confident in his decision. But time had passed. There had been a close call. Too close. And it made Preston go from willing to take a chance to knowing that he'd made the right decision in keeping himself from a relationship.

It was bad enough worrying over the twins, but if something had happened to Poppy too?

But was that selfish of him? Thinking only about himself and how he'd feel? There was also the fact that Anna and Aria loved Poppy, likely as much as he did. So, he was thinking of them. And how they'd feel if she got hurt or something happened to her because of him.

But, her leaving…that would be because of him too, wouldn't it?

The girls needed a woman in their lives. Someone who was just as clever and quick as they were. Poppy fit that order perfectly. She was an incredible woman.

"I'm feeling nervous," Poppy said softly, her voice breaking into his thoughts. He startled. She had been so quiet, he hadn't even heard her. She took a deep breath. "So, since it looks like you are still gathering your thoughts, let me share mine. Maybe…maybe it will make it easier for you."

He nodded, wondering what she would say.

"I'd already decided," Poppy said, her voice low. "I'd started to tell you that earlier." She looked away from him, and toward the window that overlooked a large tree in the yard. Right now, tiny pink flowers dotted it. Branches swayed in a gentle breeze.

"Decided." His voice was flat. He didn't know what the decision was. The sudden interruption in his study had made just about everything in the last hour turn into a jumble in his mind. Would he be able to persuade her in the opposite direction, if it was something that would make his heart ache?

"Yes." She glanced back to him, and worried her lower lip between her teeth for a moment. "I thought about it over and over, and came to the opinion that I couldn't bear the thought of being away from you. Even if that meant that I'd spend my whole life pining after you. But then you said... At least, I thought you said. That I hadn't imagined..."

Her eyes were worried, and Preston reached out, letting his hand find hers. "That I love you?"

"Yes." Her eyes were focused on his fingers.

"I do love you," he said. "Which is why I'm struggling with what to do. The smart thing or the thing I want to do."

"Which is which?" she whispered.

He thought about that. It was a good question. Did he even know the answer? After a moment, he answered. "I never thought I'd marry or have a family. It is too dangerous. I didn't want that on my conscience. The feeling grew once the girls were placed in my care. But now, after having you around, I've realized that you bring so much happiness and joy to me and the girls, I selfishly don't want to be without you."

"I don't see what's so bad about that," Poppy said, with a small smile.

"The problem is, I don't know if I can give you what you want." Preston felt tense. Anxious. He'd just realized that she cared for him, she'd said so, and he knew he loved her...but Poppy had arrived with expectations. And he was not the man she thought she was coming to marry. He hated to disappoint her.

"What do you mean?" Poppy asked. "I don't want anything more than you and the girls, and to be part of your family. Make it my family."

A pang struck his heart. That's right. She did want a family. Very much so. Poppy had been alone and on her own for so long. He wanted to pull her close, but made himself continue to express his concerns.

"But what about the travel? Would you consider still marrying me, even if I'm not the man you thought I was originally? A wealthy businessman who traveled around a lot? The truth is that I am a man who has to keep secrets sometimes, and might expose his family to danger unwillingly and unintentionally. I have some money, enough to keep us comfortable, but I am not wealthy, by any means."

"I don't care about any of that," Poppy said. She flashed him a cheeky grin. "I think the girls and I proved we can handle ourselves. As for money? I have almost all I need. What is missing in my life is the man who is standing in front of me. The loving uncle who stepped in, selflessly, to care for two little girls when he knew nothing about how to do so. A man who puts himself in danger not just for his job, but because he has a sense of justice about him.

"As for travel...who needs to travel when you have all you need here, at home? This is a lovely little town, and I expect there's much to explore nearby too. I thought travel was what I wanted, but being here has shown me that what

I wanted more than anything was to be with the people I love. You, and Anna, and Aria."

Her words brought a lump to his throat. Again, he was reminded of how this was the first time someone had wanted him for himself. Was content with what he could offer. It seemed as though she was willing to stay. But could he offer that to her? Was she speaking the truth? He desperately wanted her to be.

Poppy had been nothing but honest. Nothing but sweet and kind and content with what she had and what he offered. How could he doubt her words now? Was it because he was looking for an excuse to save himself from the terrifying feeling of letting her down?

She stepped close, and he wrapped his arms around Poppy, breathing in the scent of the vanilla fragrance she wore. He felt content having her there. Gently, he squeezed her. "There's more," he whispered. "I'm also the man who would do anything, anything at all, to make you happy. If you'll have me."

Chapter 22

Poppy thought she should have been delighted at the words she never imagined she'd hear. The words that meant a place and belonging, a family and love. But it was hard to feel those things, and the joy that she thought should have been running through her, when she saw Preston's face.

He looked so distraught, there was fear on every inch of his face. The tiny lines at the corners of his eyes seemed deeper, his complexion had an odd green tint to it, and, if she wasn't mistaken, he seemed more concerned now than when she had seen him chasing after the intruder.

Was he that worried that she would say no? She shook her head to herself. The idea was preposterous. Why, this was all that she'd wanted. Why would he think she'd say anything other than yes?

"Will you please say something?" Preston asked in a strained voice. "You are making me incredibly nervous."

Poppy gave a soft laugh and smiled at him. "Something," she teased, poking her forefinger into his chest.

Her joke had worked, and he cracked a smile. Poppy slipped her arms around his waist and rested her head on his chest. "Yes. I want you, Preston." She looked up at him. "And I will happily, and uncomplainingly accept whatever we can have. I know your job is important, and you must be away at times."

"Perhaps there will be instances that we can travel together," Preston said. "I will look into that more. There are occasions when I travel just for meetings. Those would be trips you could join me."

"That sounds wonderful," Poppy said. "I would love to travel now and again, but even if we don't, I'll be quite happy."

"And us too?" Anna's voice sounded from just outside the door.

"Could we also go?" Aria asked.

Poppy laughed as she released Preston and walked the few steps over to open the door. The girls were there, hopeful looks on their faces, and not looking the least bit ashamed.

"How long have you been standing there?" Preston asked in a scolding tone.

"Not long enough, I guess," Anna said with a small pout.

"We didn't hear if Poppy was going to be our aunt," Aria said. "You need to talk a little louder, Uncle Preston."

Anna nodded in agreement.

"Well then," Preston said with a laugh. "Let me ask her now, while you are both here so you don't miss anything." He turned to Poppy. "Miss Wilson, would you do me the honor of becoming my wife? Of staying with me and Anna and Aria forever?"

This time, Poppy didn't laugh. She didn't even smile. Instead, she fought to hold back the tears from her eyes. Emotion overwhelmed her, though, and the salty drops streamed down, as she sobbed out, "Yes, Preston, yes." And then she hugged the people who meant more to her than anyone else in the world. Her new family. People to love and cherish, and to be loved and cherished by.

Epilogue

Dahlia hummed to herself as she walked through the garden. The sunflowers were blooming nicely, and hyacinths filled the air with their fragrance. After nearly three days of rain, she was checking for any storm damage. Luckily, other than a few fallen petals, the garden had fared well.

Coming out of the house, Zinnia waved to get her attention. "We've mail!" she called.

Dahlia left the marigolds she'd been inspecting and joined her sister. She dusted off her hands. "Oh good. I love seeing who writes to us to find their happily ever after. What do we have today?"

Taking a seat at their small table, Zinnia spread the letters before them. Then she picked one up. "This name looks familiar," she said. "Oh dear! I think it's that young woman we sent to marry the man who travels. You remember? The one who didn't want a wife but a governess?"

"Open it then," Dahlia urged. "It might be her letter saying she's ready for us to find her a husband. We had promised, you know. It's been about six months, hasn't it? That was how long she'd said she'd be the governess."

Her sister nodded, and set the now-opened letter on the table between the two of them to read.

Dear Garden Belles,

I'm happy to tell you that I won't be needing a husband after all. Preston proposed to me, and last week we were married. His nieces—now also my nieces—have joined us on a short wedding trip. We traveled by train for most of a day and are in a lovely hotel. We will spend the next week walking around and taking in the sights.

You ladies did find me the perfect husband, even if he didn't think so at first! I wanted to thank you both, and let you know how things turned out. You helped me to find all that I never thought I'd have—love and a family. There is no way I can express the gratitude I feel or how happy I am.

I will be sure to tell everyone that I know you are not just matchmakers, you are dream creators.

With all my love,

Poppy Parker

"Well, that's wonderful!" Dahlia exclaimed.

"We knew they were right for each other all along," Zinnia said, a little smugly. "They just needed time to see that for themselves."

"We are good at what we do," Dahlia said. She stood from the table. "I will go make us some tea, and then let's start on today's letters. There was a young woman named Sage who wrote yesterday, and we need to find her the perfect match."

"Yes," Zinnia agreed. "I'll go fetch her letter and the others who still need to be placed together." She stood up and paused, looking at the newly arrived mail. A slow smile spread over her face as she rested her hand on the stack. "I've a good feeling about these."

Want more?

Visit the Garden Belle's Amazon page to find all the titles
in this series!

https://www.amazon.com/dp/B0CTHQJLKQ

Note from Author

Thank you for taking the time to read *Poppy*
Could I ask for one small favor? Reviews like yours on
Amazon mean so much to me and help others to find my
books! Even just a single line means a lot!

Also...

Want a FREE book?

Stop by my website to get your no strings attached **FREE
book**. It's my gift to you, as a thank you for reading this
one.

www.sarahlambbooks.com

Keep reading...

If you enjoyed this Garden Belles story, you might like my first one, *Iris*.

Iris is a handful. Liam is in dire need of a wife. But is he *that* desperate?

Iris Green doesn't mean to be such a walking disaster. Trouble just seems to find her though, and scares off all would-be suitors in the process. Unbeknown to her, her mother submits her name for a mail-order bride, thinking that's the only way she'll ever see her daughter married off.

Liam Gardener thinks it's a hoot his potential bride has a flower as her name, it's a perfect match for his last name, so it must be a good sign. However, moments after meeting her, he's regretting it something awful. Iris comes in like a whirlwind and turns his quiet life upside down, and he's not sure if he likes that.

When two very different personalities clash, will the outcome blossom into something special or will their future wilt before it even starts?

https://www.amazon.com/Iris-Garden-Belles-Mail-Orde r-Brides-ebook/dp/B0CW18918H

***

Curious about Bess from the hotel restaurant and who she almost married? Read *Joseph's Last Resort*

To protect his father's ranch from a conniving cousin, Joseph McAllen has to be married before his birthday. Unfortunately, he's almost out of time. So, he does what any desperate man would. Sends off for a mail-order answer to his prayers.

Only, when she sees him, she gets right back on the stage. Joseph never imagined he'd be rejected. Filled with desperation, he reluctantly does what he should have from the start, and sends a plea for help to his aunt Rosemary.

Too old and unwanted to be a bride herself, Ines Martin thought she'd be celebrating her younger sister's marriage in a few days. But when her sister elopes, scandal comes knocking and it's up to Ines to try and fix things when offered her own chance at wedded bliss—to a stranger.

If she accepts, Ines sees a chance to protect her parents and make her own way. The only problem is, the man isn't interested in anything but a marriage of convenience, and Ines doesn't want to be where she's not wanted.

Not one for romantic delusions, Joseph doesn't know what's worse—sophisticated and demanding Aunt Rosemary on his dusty ranch or the fact Ines might be perfect for him if he lets himself fall in love. In a clash of pride, does anyone come out the winner?

https://www.amazon.com/Josephs-Resort-Rejected-Mai l-Order-Grooms-ebook/dp/B0DPYF9J49

***

And keep an eye out for Sage's story, coming in 2026

About the Author

Sarah writes captivating characters and clean romance that's anything BUT boring! From heartbreaking moments to heartwarming tales, get swept away in either historical or small town romance that pulls you in until the last page.

Nestled in the Blue Ridge Mountains of Virginia where she's married to her Texan husband, you'll find Sarah creating her next book, homeschooling her two boys, or volunteering in her community.

Want more of Sarah's books? Find them all on Amazon!

https://www.amazon.com/stores/Sarah-Lamb/auth
or/B098H3SGLK